To Margaret and

With Best Wishes,

Liz Taylor,   November 2013

A Long Way From Eden

Previously published by Nethergate Writers

Turn Back The Cover (2007)
Roots (2008)
If Stones Could Speak (2009)
Whodunwhat (2010)
A Private View (2011)
Wheels Within Wheels (2012)

A Long Way From Eden

an anthology of new writing by Nethergate Writers

Introduction by Esther Read

Dundee
2013

First published in Great Britain in 2013 by Nethergate Writers
Website: http://nethergatewriters.webplus.net/
Email: nethergatewriters1@gmail.com

Edited by Esther Read

Cover design by Rikki O'Neill. Website: www.RIKOART.co.uk
Cover image and artwork included within the text by Jean Duncan,
www.jeaniduncan.co.uk

ISBN: 978-0-9555831-6-2

A CIP catalogue record for this book is available from the British Library

Printed and bound by CPI Group (UK) Ltd, Croydon, CR0 4YY

CONTENTS

FOREWORD

I am delighted to write this short foreword to *A Long Way From Eden*, which is the latest creative offering from the Nethergate Writers. The central motif for the group was 'a changing world and the role that people play in this process'. Whilst this may readily conjure to mind the image of the Blue Planet under pressure from a rising human population with even faster growing expectations, it can also evoke ideas of nature's amazing capacity to resist damage and recover. How we scale the future is an important concern because whilst we know there are now more people than ever before, what this means on the ground for someone on the farm or in the city is another matter altogether.

Wonderfully, the response of the writers has ranged from the direct to the abstract; from the effusive to the sardonic and from 'big picture' to the intimate and personal. Another delightful element of this collection is how many of the authors use their local Tayside environs as a canvas to explore the future, though equally there are intriguing pieces set further afield, as far indeed as West Virginia to the Australian Outback. Overall this is a wonderful and stimulating collection which resolutely defies convention and pigeon-holing. Enjoy!

October, 2013
Professor John Rowan
Director, Centre for Environmental Change and Human Resilience,
University of Dundee

ACKNOWLEDGEMENTS

A Long Way from Eden is the seventh book from Nethergate Writers and no doubt readers will make their own judgements on the talent, imagination and literary value within its pages. We tend to associate books with their writers – and rightly so. The writers, however, would be first to acknowledge the parts played by other members of the team in helping to make *A Long Way from Eden* a success.

Nethergate Writers is the book publishing arm of the 'Continuing as Writer' courses offered by Continuing Education at the University of Dundee and our sincere thanks are due to Kaye Stevenson and her colleagues for their ongoing support.

Rikki O'Neill, whose eye-catching and imaginative cover designs have enhanced our previous six books, has again excelled himself and richly deserves our thanks.

In addition to looking after our finances Ed Thompson has again taken on the thankless task of proof-reading while our Secretary, Amanda Barclay, has added her invaluable contribution to the mix. *A Long Way from Eden* was inspired by the work of the Centre for Environmental Change and Human Resilience based in Dundee and we are very much indebted to its Director, Professor John Rowan, for his support and input along with that of Jean Duncan, the Centre's artist-in-residence.

Finally tribute must be paid to our Class Tutor, Esther Read. With her usual imagination and energy she encouraged the writers to identify and develop the stories and poetry that are *A Long Way from Eden*. In addition she managed the project from the initial discussion stage as the 2013 Project through to final printing and marketing where it took on its shiny new identity as *A Long Way from Eden*.

Stuart Wardrop,
Chair, Nethergate Writers.

INTRODUCTION

Esther Read

If you've ever wanted to write fiction but don't know where to start, try putting a character into a given situation and then ask, 'What if such-and-such happened? What would my character do?' You may be surprised at the range of possibilities open to you.

Certainly that proved to be the case for the writers involved in *A Long Way From Eden*. Following a presentation by Professor John Rowan, Director of the Centre for Environmental Change and Human Resilience (CECHR) at the University of Dundee, they were sent off to ponder the question, 'What if… climate change?' The responses were as various as the characters they devised, though their own views on the issue clearly influenced their choices.

A surprising number found humour in the subject – everything from farce to satire. Try *Tribunal* by Ed Thompson, *Major Incident and the Mooshiners* by Roddie McKenzie, *La Vita è Bella* by June Cadden, *Feeding Time* by Ann-Marie Aslen, *Tay Beavers* by Roderick Manson and *Hughie's Bad Day* by Nan Rice – while the final (though none too definitive word) goes to *Earth Summit* by Ward McGaughrin.

Some went to the other extreme and foresaw the future in apocalyptic terms yet humans still strive to survive. The question then becomes – at what cost? Those who took up the challenge of providing an answer include Fiona Duncan with *The House*, Helen Taylor with *Ancients* and Fiona Pretswell with *Seaweed and Cotton*.

Others adopted a global perspective, recognising that climate change happens across borders and continents, but that climate is not the only factor impacting on the environment. Politics, economics and the mores of a particular society also play their part. Illustrating this, we have stories set as far afield as Africa, Iceland, the USA and Australia. See *Who Owns This Land?* by Jessma Carter, *Lost Mountain* by Deborah Williams-Kurz, *Ezekiel* by Stuart Wardrop, *A Lovely Day for an Airstrike* by C.B. Donald and *Wind of Change* by Joyce McKinney.

Yet the implications of climate change are always going to seem most pressing when they strike close to home. How are we, in Scotland, and in Britain as a whole, going to be affected and how might we respond to the challenges? Two of the writers, Cathy Whitfield and Hamish McBride, graphically illustrate the impact

1

of climate change on individuals in *Moving On* and *Snow*. Others, including Ann Prescott in *Hot Air* and Catherine Maidment in *Lovage Soup*, suggest practical approaches to the problem, while the character in *Good Neighbours* by Linda Louden has her own solution, though it's not necessarily a socially desirable one.

What is and what is not socially desirable is also at the heart of *Tilting at Windmills* by David Carson, *Roots* by Janice Thomson and *Earth Mither* by Elizabeth Taylor, while for something completely different you might care to try the flight of fancy that is *The Cat and the Corn* by J. Stirling.

Ultimately, however, the real spur to responding wisely to the challenges posed by climate change may be to value and celebrate the landscape we have as Roderick Manson and Chris Smith do in the reflective *Luing* and the elegiac *The River*.

We are privileged in this particular anthology to have the work of Jean Duncan R.U.A., artist-in-residence at CECHR, illustrated in the book. Jean's work offers her own distinctive view of the environment yet may also be cross-referenced with some of the writing to be found here. Taken as a whole I am confident that *A Long Way From Eden* not only offers the usual entertaining mix that readers have come to expect from Nethergate Writers but will provide a jumping-off point for discussion of one of the most urgent and controversial issues of our time. So, for example, if *you* were to be the character in one of the 'given situations' outlined in any of the stories, how would you react?

WHO OWNS THIS LAND?

Jessma Carter

Zimbabwe

The perfection of yesterday evening's golden horizon had gone. The calm, the night whisperings, the long, deep, dark rest of the land had gone. Harare was awake and big and noisy and greedy and the sun was brutal. Angus had urged me to come when he heard of my business trip to South Africa. "Like old times, James. When we were kids. Come on up to Zim, man." I had no particular memory of his being a bosom buddy but I was curious to get the feel of Zimbabwe so I agreed to visit.

I was strolling around while I waited and had noticed the boy and his strange machine. It was like a very large tricycle with what looked like an old dustbin fixed at the front. A battered car seat was fitted between the two wheels at the back and an umbrella had been extended and was tied to the dustbin at the front. It was a working miracle made from scrap. People came up to the boy and he delved into the bin and held up a magazine or a paper. He had the loose body of a teenager, with limbs that looked too long. When he pushed his machine across to me, I could see that one of the boy's legs was shorter and thinner than the other but his smile was huge and frank and fearless.

"Any magazines? Any papers for you today, sir?"

"No, thank you. I am waiting for a friend. Perhaps later, when I come back."

"Are you a visitor? Are you American?"

"No. Scottish."

His smile became a hearty laugh as he slapped his knees with his hands. "Scottish. I know Scotland very well." I was intrigued. "Yes. Scotland is like Zimbabwe. We are brothers. Scotland and Zimbabwe. We have never been defeated by Julius Caesar."

"What's your name?" I was smiling.

"Yesterday is my name."

He could see my face and laughed again and slapped his legs in pure joy. "This is true. Yesterday is my name. I was born late and my mother said

3

to me, 'You should have been here yesterday'. Now she says I will always remember not to be late."

We were both laughing as Angus came up to us apologising for his lateness. "I see you've met Yesterday. You haven't been selling my friend any ancient magazines, have you?"

Yesterday was affronted. "Ancient? Sir. Sir. These are magazines no more than one week old. Look here. Just one week old." He pulled one out of his bin and held it up.

Angus got hold of my arm and pulled me away. "The transport is just round the corner here."

I can still smell the street corner where Angus and I met. The street lined with Jacaranda trees, blue flowers open and oily in a last bid for survival, a layer of scent in the motionless air, but what had once been fragrance was now almost choking sweetness. The early morning breeze speckled gray from exhaust fumes. Business was up and running and with it the clatter of old cars, the shouts of workers running after an already filled city-cab, the laughter around banana sellers, unbearable heat from corn roasters. It was here, on Fifth Street, that the suburbs became city. It was here that those walking many miles into work took their shoes from where they had hung laced together round their necks and put them on their respectable feet. It was here that mothers stroked the faces of their pretty daughters and turned away as the girls made their way to the railway station. They would travel all week in the squeal of the train, selling themselves, pliant and grateful as the carriages moved across barren, lonely lands to South Africa. It was here at the street corner where international companies shouted out their presence on the skyline.

Angus was even bigger and bronzer than when we had met briefly a couple of years before at his brother's funeral in Scotland. We had played together as boys, for my father had worked on his father's farm. We had lived in one of the farm cottages and we sat together at primary school. It had been easy to drift apart. Angus had gone to agricultural college and the next thing I heard was that he had bought a farm in Zimbabwe and was 'doing well'. Now he must be like me, near retirement age. The transport was a big four-by-four which he drove with skill, using the tips of his large fingers to turn the steering wheel, easily manoeuvring around the small cars belching black fumes, many with no doors.

"Spare parts not easy to come by. Unless…" he flicked his fingers indicating bribery.

The size of the apple shed took me aback. I knew one farm could stretch from Perth to Dundee, but the vast packing shed, the tables and tables of women packing apples was awe-inspiring. Behind each table was a pile of apples that were continually being renewed as tractors spilled their contents. Beside each woman was a blackboard with the days of the week and series of ticks beside each day. Another board named last week's champion packer – Atashe. The women were singing, a quiet slow murmur, sometimes a voice calling, but nothing seemed hurried. They lifted each apple carefully, turned it gently like they held a rosy world in their hands and then put it on a tray. The work seemed easy and pleasant, the smell of apples enticing. Occasionally one woman would throw an apple into a cardboard box, her arm moving to the rhythm of the song.

"Do the workers get the bruised ones?"

Angus had left me with his manager, Mr George, to show me around. "Not at all. The animals get them. The men would make beer with them and we don't want that." He watched my reaction and then quickly added, "This farm here is good for families, very good. We have men in the fields and the women in the packing sheds. The families all have a house specially built and there is a school for the children."

It sounded paternal and kind but I could sense a sales pitch. I looked again carefully at the manager – he was young and black. From Bulawayo, he told me, educated in college in South Africa. So what was he hiding, wary of saying? I wandered around the shed, speaking to the women about the apples, what kind? When the apples were harvested what next? A bell rang out and we went out to the glare of the sun. Small children were standing wide-eyed, slightly anxious, watching for their mums, hiding in their skirts as they walked back to the compound for a meal. Mr George came after me with an eager invitation to meet the families. "You will meet Atashe, sir. She is the best worker. You will see her house, her family. She will be proud to show you." He scurried along beside me. "Follow me, sir. You will see for yourself how we treat our workers."

The compound had perhaps twenty houses. They had been built by the workers themselves – single brick, with a corrugated iron roof, about the size of a small garage divided into two rooms. At the back was a toilet and shower room. Outside was a water tap and a place for a fire. Atashe's father was poking twigs into the fire. Against the wall was a pile of twigs and branches that he had brought from the bush.

Atashe was a tall woman by African standards, very slim with delicate hands. She seemed to sense the world with her hands for she touched everything

5

as she spoke. "This is my father who is too old to work. He gathers the wood and he watches the chickens while I sort apples for Mr Tesco." Atashe stroked his head and shoulders as she spoke. "And this here is my mother." Both father and mother were busy at the stove, he keeping the fire going, she stirring a pot of meal and what looked like gravy.

I was pleased to see Yesterday come out of the house grinning at me. "I know this man," he said to his mother. "This man is a Scotch man."

"Does your father work on the farm?" I asked him but it was his mother who replied. She covered her face with her hands and moaned, "My husband is dead, sir."

Mr George explained, "Atashe's husband was killed in the same accident that injured Yesterday. But she is allowed to have her parents here to help her."

"Was it here on the farm?" I spoke to Atashe.

"It was here. We were all busy, busy. It was bad, very bad. A tractor fell over. Yesterday was ten years old. Now he can't work on the farm but he sells papers. One day he will be rich. I know that for I am saving money for him to go to school in town."

"But there is a school here on the farm?"

"For small children. When they are big, they need to go to town."

Angus and his wife entertained me well. A couple of sundowners, a side of beef and more wine than I could cope with. Angus lived entirely in a man's world and was proud of it. After dinner we went to his over-furnished sitting room. There he smoked 'good Rhodesian tobacco' as he reached for the whisky decanter.

"A favour to ask of you, old son." Angus handed me a large tumbler as he sat down on a couch opposite.

"Yes?"

"I've got this money here. Maybe you could just send it off to my bank in Jersey when you get back to the UK?"

I was slow to catch on. "Are things so bad you have no access to a bank?"

"Sure. Sure. But you understand, you must have heard, Mugabe and his boys don't want money going out of the country. Unless they take it, that is."

"I'm to smuggle it?"

"More or less."

"How much?"

"About £100,000."

"What's going on here?"

6

Angus inhaled deeply, sat up straight and spoke to me as to a child. "You've got to understand. I won't last long here. Soon one of Mugabe's henchmen is going to come and take me over, lock, stock and barrel. You understand? I'm retiring back to Scotland and I need some capital. They're beginning to suspect me."

"And the workers? What will happen to them?"

Angus shook his head in despair. "You don't get it, do you? I've put forty years of my life into this place, don't I deserve something back? After I go, the farm can rot for all I care."

He was his father. I saw again the arrogance of ownership. I saw again the great bitterness that almost choked my father when he was told to leave his tied cottage. "He promised me, the swine, gave his word that after forty years he'd let me stay. I've never cheated him out of even an hour's work all my life. The swine." I could see him still, that shake of his head, that sigh, the way he gripped the arm of the chair when he muttered over and over, "I never cheated him. I never would." He blew into a handkerchief. "You get some crafty buggers. Remember that, son. All out for themselves."

Angus was still in full flow. "Everybody's got to survive. You got that? I built up this farm. I gave these people jobs. I gave them houses. I feed them." He waggled his fingers at me. "These lazy black bastards get a bag of meal every week and they can eat as many fucking chickens as they can raise. I pay them $35 a month and the likes of Atashe can add another $5 or $6 dollars if she gets a badge from Mr Tesco for packing the most apples. I did that for them."

There was silence for a while then his mood changed quickly. As a boy, he had shouted down any questioning of his assertions and taken it as victory when we walked quietly away from him. That night we went to bed in a fuzz of late night aimless chat. If there was rancour, it was on my side. It was primitive. It was atavistic.

I took the envelope and the bank account number, tucked them in the inside pocket of my jacket. Mr George was driving me to the airport and we talked little, for the ride was bumpy and the radio was crackling loudly. There was an air of hostility in the airport lounge and the many police, while looking impassive, carried well-polished guns. Angus had assured me that I would not be questioned as he would have been for carrying a lot of money but I was very aware of the packet on my chest. As an inferior, Angus was sure I would do his bidding. In the departure lounge several young women were shaking tins and boxes, asking for money. "Any loose change, sir? Anything at all? For orphans, for teachers for our orphans? Tariro is a charity, sir. For children."

I looked up at the girl. She wasn't asking for much. She wasn't expecting much. "Here," I said, and took the envelope out of my jacket pocket. "Take this." I walked through the open door onto the tarmac and straight into the plane, expecting a shout, the girl to come running after me, asking if I had made a mistake.

From the air, the land was sand-coloured scrub and leafless trees, herds of giraffe bounded underneath the noise of the plane. Rain was coming from the north and we flew towards the great grey clouds. Some riverbeds were dry and being used as roadways but the Zambezi was still moving strongly. Cattle lumbered, sniffing the air, waiting for rain. Orchards were stripped and the fruits off to Europe. And underneath this dried land, great rocks and pools held water in trust; silver and gold and copper were waiting to be plundered.

Below me, still waiting for the benison of rain, Zimbabwe was disappearing.

FLOW

Catherine Young

Spring

She was early. He was late. She noted his mud spattered Landrover crunched to a halt next to the picnic table, not in one of the eight designated parking spaces. She recognised him straight away of course and watched in her rear view mirror as he got out of his Landrover with a practiced little leap. He walked around to the passenger side and gently lifted down a brown and white spaniel from the seat. It looked up at him, tail wagging and didn't leave his side. She practised a smile in the mirror.

She watched as he unloaded an armful of stuff from the back of the vehicle and plonked it on the picnic table. He yanked on a filthy looking Barbour jacket over a fleece, rummaged around for a battered A4 envelope that he stuffed into his back pocket and threw the rest of the detritus back into the Landrover.

Suddenly he was striding towards her Fiat Panda. She zipped up her mountain jacket and grabbed at her clipboard on the passenger seat but the case for her reading glasses slid off onto the floor. She reached for it but her seatbelt was still buckled.

He knocked on the car window.

"Oh, just a minute!" She grappled for the belt buckle and unhooked herself, bumped her head on the rear view mirror and missed the glasses' case.

"Why don't I get that for you?" He reached for the passenger door but it was locked.

"Got it." She gathered her things together. Her notebook was still open with her yellow post-it listing three bullet points on how to tackle the meeting. She placed her glasses' case on top but couldn't tell if he'd read *Follow plan. Keep it short. Concrete action points.*

"Hello." He reached out his hand but she clutched the clipboard to her chest.

"Sorry, sorry, run out of hands."

He stood a little awkwardly. "It's good to see you back in the village again. Though obviously not in the circumstances. We were all really sad to hear…"

"Please. I can't talk about it." She raised a navy-gloved hand, now suddenly

9

free of encumbrance. "As you know," she rushed, as she locked her car, "I've been asked to take over the quarterly review of the common and pathways for the community steering group."

"Yeah, how did they manage to rope you into this?"

"Well, it's a bit of extra money." She took a breath. "Look I understand there's been a fairly ad hoc arrangement so far between the group and you as landowner but with funding bodies getting involved now we need to have a more rigorous structure to how we operate."

"Do you not just want to go for a walk along the path and take a look?"

"Yes, yes." She opened her clipboard. "I've prepared a checklist, you might want to…" but he'd thrown a stick for the dog and strode off in front of her, the mud spraying up over the back of his trousers in a fine mist.

In the car park section of the checklist she wrote down 'muddy underfoot'.

She was only a few metres along the riverside walk when she stopped. Brambles splayed over the path. "This is a real hazard. Can we clear this?"

He walked back, tugged his jacket sleeve down to cover his hand and pulled at the bramble stems, tucking them behind a nearby tree trunk.

"There you go. Hopefully that'll do the trick."

Her pen hovered over the form. "I really think cutting them might…"

"We'd get lynched if there weren't any brambles come autumn."

"True. There used to be rasps as well somewhere. We used to stuff our faces when we came up for sausage sizzles with the Brownies." Her voice trailed off and she looked down at the clipboard, put a query at the obstacles box and carried on walking.

A little later he asked, "Do people actually want the burn and common to be quite so organised? The whole point is you come here to get away from it all for a while. You need some fresh air to blow away the cobwebs. Let your mind wander. If people wanted to walk on neat wee paths they could stay in the village."

She didn't reply.

"What the hell is wrong with getting your boots a bit muddy anyway?"

She looked down. Her new Gore-Tex walking boots were filthy. She wrote 'muddy boots'.

Summer

She was early. He was only a few minutes late this time. She noted he parked his Landrover next to the picnic table again, though there was about half of the parking spaces still available.

He did the same little leap out and walked around to lift the dog from the passenger seat. He was in shirtsleeves for their summer review. His arms and face were already tanned. She still had her mountain jacket on. She pulled the zip down a few inches from her chin. This time she was ready and was locking her car just as he reached her.

She looked over her shoulder. "Hello. All set?"

His right hand hovered then he put it in his jeans pocket. He nodded. "Looks like a better day."

As they started to walk she inched down her jacket zip a little, then tugged it back up. She'd put her bullet points on a piece of white paper this time rather than a yellow post-it. *Discuss further flooding improvements and prettying up.*

"Prettying up?" he laughed. "How is whapping decking on top of all those marsh flowers pretty? If it didn't flood you wouldn't get all these flowers. Isn't that the whole point of coming for a walk here? Surely it's worth taking the risk of a wee bit flooding for this?" He pointed expansively. "What we've got here is fairly rare you know."

She didn't expect him to be so passionate about wildflowers or maybe he was just against the decking. She didn't know how to respond.

"Remember that class project we did up here?" He stopped and turned to face her. "Didn't you win an art prize or something for those paintings of the wildflowers? Why don't you get them printed up on wee plaques so everyone knows what they're trampling on?"

A blush surged up over her throat, neck and into her cheeks. She'd forgotten all about the art prize. Imagine him remembering. There were a lot of flowers. She hadn't been up for a walk on her own since she'd returned to the village. She was just wondering if she was too late to see some of the Purple Orchids when he splashed into the burn up ahead of her.

"Something's got a bit stuck here." Water had pooled and seeped over the banking and flooded the walkway. He tugged at a broken branch in the burn with all sorts of debris collecting around it.

"Can you kick some of that away?" He motioned to the leaves and dirt blocked around the branch. She dipped the toe of her boot in the water and nudged the clogged leaves as he continued to pull. Suddenly with a gush, the branch came loose and the water rushed on, taking all the debris with it.

He turned and smiled, wiping his wet hands on his jeans. "That's cleared it. Back to flowing freely again."

Autumn

She parked in the space closest to the picnic table. She was still reversing straight when he arrived in his Landrover and drew up next to her car.

She smiled briefly. "Hello. I thought we might discuss the latest ideas for the funding applications."

He raised his eyebrows. "Oh, aye? Maybe we could apply for a Lottery Grant to get a whole bunch of wellies instead of carpeting the place with more decking. That's my idea. Give the wild flowers at least a bit of a fighting chance. We could have a box at the road end with rows of wellies all different sizes, numbers painted on their sides like bowling shoes at the bowling alley."

"Most people don't do a circular walk, how would you return them when you were finished?"

"OK, so two wee boxes one either end. Maybe we could create a job – part-time wellie coordinator with special responsibility for mud cleaning."

She scribbled 'wellie coordinator!' in the margins of the checklist and tried to hide a smirk.

As the path narrowed, he took a step in front. Mud was half way up the back of his trousers. She remembered watching the same thing after they'd been dropped off by the school bus years before. Once mud had got as far as the shoulder of his school blazer though she was never quite sure if it was sprayed up from his walking or how he swung his black Adidas bag, chopping at the hedgerow.

He was doing the same now, gently thwacking her draft report against the tall grasses as they walked along the riverbank. He hadn't really changed from that gawky schoolboy. Rounder maybe. Not fat, not even overweight. Just his features were a bit softer.

She returned to her checklist. "Historically there's been a real problem with flooding. For example the summer of 2012 apparently. That's why there's the proposal for more duckboards."

"The reason the flooding was so bad then was because the ground was already saturated before the rain. The water table was full. Best just to let the burn burst its banks, seep over and flood on the natural flood plain where it's always done."

"I know it might not look like we're doing a lot," he continued, "but this didn't just happen. The barrier alleviates things like nitrate run off."

"Mmm," she raised her eyebrows. "It also means when the burn floods it naturally edges out without spoiling your crops."

He smiled. "Yeah well, and the community gets their path along the river with all these different flowers and wildlife. Bit of a win-win. You know we can mitigate against the worst but for the rest, you just have to kind of…"

"Go with the flow?" she offered.

"Well, yes," he smiled. "Can't control everything. It's nature. Don't see what's wrong with getting your boots a bit muddy now and again anyway."

"I believe that was the explanation you gave the first time we came up here. See, it's in my notes, 'muddy boots'."

"Want to know what's in my notes from then?"

"Notes?"

"All up here," he pointed to his slightly greying temple. "Definitely needs to roll down the hill shouting 'Weee!' again like when we were kids. It wasn't till the summer visit that I first saw you smile. Getting covered in all that sticky willie, remember?"

"In my notes as, profusion of Galium Aparine, part of the Rubiaceae (Bedstraw) family, partially impeding walkers."

"Aye, right."

It was his deadpan delivery that did it. That wee twitch around his lips. She was never quite sure if what he was saying was innocuous or playful and flirting. There wasn't quite a twinkle in his eye but there was something waiting to burst out if it got the slightest encouragement, or even acknowledgement. She could sense an opportunity to flirt was being offered but not the actual flirt itself. It could all be taken at a very serious po-faced level if she really wanted to. It was clearly being left up to her. Or was she reading far, far too much into a perfectly innocent situation?

"Great, the brambles are finally ready." He pulled a couple of berries from a trailing branch and handed them to her.

The soft berries gave way, their dark juice staining her fingers before she popped them into her mouth.

He started wading into the bushes growing up the small embankment. "There's a load hiding up the back here."

"Watch yourself," she said as his foot slid on the mud. The sleeve of his Barbour jacket snagged on the bramble branch. He freed himself then licked his bleeding hand.

"Is it worth it for a few handfuls of berries?"

"Oh aye. It's the quest. Men like a challenge." He laughed and piled brambles into a beanie hat he'd dragged from one of his pockets. "Got enough here to make a wee pot of jam if I mix it with some windfall apples."

FLOW

"You make jam?"

He nodded.

"Well that's something I didn't know about you. Mrs Milne in third year Home Ec. would be proud."

"You'd be surprised what you can do if you put your mind to it."

Winter

He'd texted to say he'd collect her in his Landrover. "That wee Fiat of yours'll make a right hash of it in the snow," he'd said by way of explanation.

As they passed the picnic table he scooped up a handful of snow and tossed a snowball in front of them. The dog scampered looking for it, his paws getting lost with each step.

The flurry of snow excited her. She felt alive. On an adventure. A very small adventure but still, an adventure. She'd been closeted up in the house for so long. Everything far too cosy. She felt like Sherpa Tenzing padding up the incline, making footprints in the virgin snow which crêpe-crêped with each step. It was dry and white, not slippy underfoot. She stepped out rather confidently using walking poles. This was nothing like negotiating the grey slush and ruts on the village pavements.

The wind buffeted her hood against the right side of her face. Her fleece hat kept riding forward as her hood moved and she folded it up at the front so she could see. The right side of her face was tingling in the cold snow; the left was cocooned under the layers of hood and fleecy hat. Her hearing had also gone oddly mono; muted on one side, shrill and acute on the other. She looked at the backs of his trousers; snow was clinging to the fabric up to his knees.

They walked in silence, the snow muffling their steps. As they turned off the boardwalk and back to the car park he put his hand on her arm and gently pulled her towards him. "Look there." He nodded to their right. A robin was landing on a snow-covered holly branch and behind was the white lacework of a frosty cobweb.

"Perfect timing. Couldn't have made it up if you tried." He slowly reached into his pocket for his phone and took a photo. He sheltered the screen from the snow with his arm as they peered at it together.

"Ideal for next year's Christmas card."

She nodded.

When they got back to the car park, he opened up the back of the Landrover and got out a steel thermos, two cups, bread and a small pot of bramble jam.

She started clearing some snow from the top of the picnic table, looked up at him, smiled, then quickly pushed some into a snowball and threw it. It burst square on his chest.

EARTH MITHER'S RANT

Elizabeth Taylor

Hoo can A cairry on this wey?
A dinnae get nae time tae rest.
A'm warkin aa the oors God gies,
year in, year oot, an that's nae lees.
Nae suiner has the combine cam
tae bale an bind an gaither in,
than there's the fairmer wi his ploo,
an stibble raws turned ower tae broon.
An then, b'God, he's plantin mair –
neeps, rape seed, oats or barley meal,
an A'm supposed tae mak them graw
while snaws pile up, an snell winds blaw!
He'll mebby spread a bit o muck
an say A'm aw Organic like,
but maistly it's jist secks o lime
an nitrates, phosphates – aa the time.
O, Lord A'michty, hoo can A
keep goin on aa seasons roond
athoot some chance tae catch ma breath?
They'll wear me oot. A'll catch ma death.
A've fed them aa since time began –
the Picts, the Scots, the Normans tae.
Thon Roman legions focht fir me.
Thi've aa jist thocht it cam fir free.
But Auld Yins kent, come Winter's blast
until the licht's begun tae stretch,
it wis ma time tae coorie doon
an rest aneath the Hervest moon.

So learn frae them, an think o me.
A'm gey near puggled, so A am.
You fowks'll no ken whit tae dae
wance A'm nae mair, an aa's aglee.

LOST MOUNTAIN

Deborah Williams-Kurz

Joey didn't know how to 'nail his butt to the seat'. He tried, but Bill kept thwacking him on the head with his stylus and he just had to smack him back. It wasn't fair, not his fault. He struggled to focus, but couldn't catch his breath so he stood up to get Ms Johnston's attention.

"I need my inhaler," he wheezed.

Joey's teacher let out a poorly concealed sigh and punched in the code that unlocked the cabinet packed with medical paraphernalia. She parroted the routine phrase. "We'll start with two puffs and see how it goes."

Breathing freely again, Joey sat back down and stuck his tongue out at Bill, who tried to pull his chair out from under him. Bill was just jealous that Joey could get out of his chair.

Writing about his weekend was so boring. Joey couldn't care less. He glanced out the grimy window at the tall white silo. Beyond the silo lay Coal Ride Mountain. The squat brick building, Stubbs Elementary School, sat in the shadow of Coal Ride, which looked like the moon, grey and pocked with holes. He imagined himself floating above it, landing on its surface, planting his flag on its dam.

His dad had told Joey stories about hunting deer on Coal Ride. "Back when the trees were thick on the mountain, we'd spend the day hiking. We even swam in the stream." Joey couldn't imagine what swimming wild would be like.

Now Joey's dad stayed home most days. He'd lost his job when the mine switched owners. The new company decided to blow the top right off the mountain, so they took the miners out from underground. But they only needed a couple of men to harvest the coal after that. Dad and most of his friends ended up on unemployment. Joey heard from the old timers in town that they had blasted nearly 800 feet off of Coal Ride. He wished he'd been around to see the explosion.

During recess, the children played Dam Break. When the older boys yelled, "Break!" everyone ran for the high ground by the fence. The kids in wheelchairs had to watch from the pavement and were called 'the goners'. Sidon Elementary only had three minutes to get away when their dam broke. Joey didn't like to think of all those boys and girls stuck in the black water. They didn't know what was coming for them. That's why they hadn't made it. That wouldn't happen at Stubbs.

"Top of the mountain!" Joey yelled, reaching the highest point. The kids who hadn't made it to the top yet yelled back, "Bottom of the valley!" Joey didn't know much about the hidden valley. After all, the gorge had been filled in ages ago. The dirt from Coal Ride Mountain had been dumped into the valley and the stream that ran behind the school was buried in the process. Joey knew that the kids used to go fishing back there after school.

Though Joey wasn't first to the top, he was fast enough. He'd be able to climb the hill across the road from the school when the dam broke. Joey figured he could beat the slurry. Just now, though, he needed another puff so he headed towards the classroom. Ms Johnston used her whole hand to slam the door button, all along never taking her eyes off Joey. She knew immediately what he needed and headed for the cabinet, bringing him the inhaler.

Joey's mom had blamed the dust for his asthma. She had always said it "tickled her lungs, more than a cigarette ever could." He didn't understand what that meant. She never was a smoker. Sure she had tried it, she said, but it wasn't for her. But that hadn't helped her lungs. They gave out anyway.

When Ms Johnston let Joey back out, she glanced around the playground and yelled at the Peck twins, "Stay away from that pipe!" The boys quickly looked at each other, then their teacher. They turned and ran towards the grass. Water dribbled from the pipe, staining the surrounding rocks a terracotta red. The children liked to throw rocks in the trickle to see how long it took for them to turn colour.

A group of girls were using the oddly coloured stones as markers in their hopscotch game. Jenny had the best rock. Hers was huge and practically neon orange. She always had the best stone since she was the number one hopscotch player. The boys hunted through the stones when Ms Johnston wasn't looking, hoping to find one of the rare blue ones. They called these 'robin eggs' and traded them with each other for sweets at lunch. The older boys thought they were funny and called the robin eggs 'rock candy'.

When the bell rang Joey walked over to Bill. Everyone was assigned a goner to push back into the classroom, so he was stuck dealing with annoying Bill all the time. It started raining so Joey pushed as quickly as he could, but Bill was just so heavy. The two boys were last in the room. Bill called him a 'wimpy wiener', which made everyone at Joey's table laugh. Last thing he needed was another nickname. He glanced over at Jenny. She had heard Bill and was laughing along with the rest of the table. Joey kicked Bill in the shins, as his cheeks warmed.

THE LOST MOUNTAIN

Ms Johnston called for the boys and girls to take a seat and be quiet. She started a history lesson on the early settlers in Appalachia. She said something about the "hardy Ulster Scots" who were used to living in the mountains and who wouldn't let anyone take their land. Joey's eyelids kept on flapping down, but Ms Johnston just went on and on. Blah, blah, blah, hard work. Blah, blah, blah, tough life. She pulled up pictures of shabby little log cabins on everybody's screens and went on; something about patchwork quilts from old clothes and nothing wasted.

"Wake up!" Joey heard Ms Johnston, right by his ear, followed by another round of laughter. This was not his day.

That was when the flood warning began, ringing through the school, drowning Joey in sound. Even though he wasn't supposed to, he reached for his coat. After all, he had two robin eggs buttoned in the pocket. He took a hold of the handles on Bill's chair and moved into the line. The children followed Ms Johnston out to the flood drill spot where she worked her head up and down, matching faces to the names on her list.

The forecast was for rain: days and days of rain. The weather bureau had put out flood warnings for most of West Virginia. Mudslides were likely, what with there being so few trees. Someone should have told those trees to nail their butts to their seat, Joey chuckled. He had the rest of the week off of school while a board of very important people 'assessed the situation'. In the meantime, he was free to play video games all he wanted. Joey couldn't believe his luck. It looked like it was going to be his day after all. Heck, it was going to be his week.

TRIBUNAL

ED THOMPSON

The day this one began, there wasn't much happening around the world, and even less locally, so the boss sent me out to find a story on my own. A golden opportunity for a young reporter, he said. Easy for him. In his day you could go down to the harbour, find out the time of High Tide, and build yourself a reputation as an investigative journalist. And that was before the ice melted and the sea-level began to rise.

Did I mention it was raining? Well it was. So I tried to keep out of it by phoning round A & E, Traffic, Regional Crime, Lifeboats; but all I got was rubbish jokes. As usual, my Forensics contact was the corniest. Anyway, they had nothing to tell, nothing to sell. So I had to do like the boss said, and get out onto the mean streets. Well, they used to be mean, before the beggars, winos, junkies and other human toxic waste were cleared away. Clean and tidy now, but still depressingly wet.

The rain wasn't all that bad, really. Just about average for the time of the year. Enough to mist up my spectacles, though, and that's how I came to misread the sheet in the High Court building and ended up covering a hearing of the Environment Tribunal. With my rain-pixillated specs I thought the notice said Employment Tribunal.

So I eased into the Press Box. It was empty, so I doubled up the cushions to combat the flat-pack arse syndrome, wiped my specs, and took a look round. To be fair, it was pretty much like an employment tribunal. A couple of lawyer-types sat in the middle of the courtroom, playing with their expenses sheets.

There was the usual three monkeys arrangement on the Bench. The one in the middle had to be the Chairman. He looked to be some sort of senior civil servant – a technocrat, not quite smooth and pink enough to be a politico, more like the headmaster from hell, eyes narrowed over little half-moon spectacles perched halfway down his nose. On his right there was a very large woman with long straight hair; she was dressed entirely in black, and had career Trade Union written all over her. The third member of the tribunal had the tired suit and standard white stubble you see on men from Social Work. The men who love to say *No*. As the hearing progressed I realised I had got him wrong. He must have been some sort of environment appointment. B.Sc. in Agrimony or somesuch.

There was no-one at the table where the accused usually sits, but down in front of the Bench was a thin little man in a dusty black gown and glossy white wig. Nylon, maybe, or something like Lurex. Synthetic, anyway, so not a barrister. Besides, he was facing sideways to the Tribunal. I figured him for the Clerk of the Court.

Like I say, the standard set-up. No, not quite. The public area was empty – usually there's a bunch of schoolchildren in there researching a Civics project. I decided to give it half an hour or so, time at least to get warm and dry. There was a minuscule chance I might turn up a story. Maybe somebody was trying to slip something through on the Q.T. – like putting up a turbine or a block of affordable housing in a garden of remembrance.

The hearing was already under way. A heavy-set man with a lived-in face was giving evidence. He was wearing a dark shirt crossed by a well-polished Sam Browne belt. Apparently a random check of somebody's blue bin had flagged up a problem. *Random?* I thought, *Gimme a break!* It would be a bunch of Young Greens getting their whistle-blowing badges. Don't get me wrong, the YGs have done a great job in getting litter and chewing gum off the streets. If they've had to hand out a few fat lips on the way, that's okay by me. No-one can deny we need a disciplined approach to the environment. But – well, I had been hoping for something like dog fouling, which is always good for a filler in the evening edition. I didn't relish going to the editor with BLUE BIN DRAMA. MAN HELD.

Anyhow this guy was banging on about how one of their snap checks had flagged up an unacceptably high ratio of metal to paper in a wheelie bin at a certain address. A fingertip search had been authorised and they found a lot of leaflets and catalogues which had not had their metal staples removed. And there was more. The searchers found that window envelopes had been put into the paper bin without first removing the plastic.

So what's so bad about that, I was thinking. For this you haul some poor citizen before an Environmental Tribunal? I began to think there might just be a story here, a human interest piece about some pensioner, maybe a bit forgetful, maybe just a bit short-sighted, with arthritic hands – I could just see the photo of his tired, wrinkled old face – getting harassed by over-zealous Greenshirts. Hit with a hefty fine or a custodial. But then the witness said that the staples had not been removed from *any* of the material in the bin, and the little plastic window had not been removed from *any* of the envelopes. Plus there was foil and bubblewrap tucked away under the legitimate paper. Being a balanced reporter, I could see where the prosecution was coming from. Like the man said, this showed signs of being intentional.

This was when one of the lawyers put aside her doodling and joined in. I imagine that she was an advocate for the defence, appointed by the Tribunal because the accused was not present in person. Apparently she was not comfortable about the Tribunal attributing motive to the accused. Granted that the alleged behaviour of the accused might *seem* criminal, no evidence had been presented as to *why* the accused behaved in this way.

The Chairman was quick to respond, so quick I wondered if the advocate's question had not been rehearsed in advance. "The evidence we have heard points to a deliberate flouting of the law," he snapped. "And let us be clear, it is a very reasonable law. We do not ask every citizen to –" he paused, as though searching for an appropriate illustration "– to compost his nail clippings, for example. This is laudable, but it is a matter of personal choice. But there is no room whatsoever for choice in the recycling of household materials for which specific provision has been made and is established by law. Where such household waste is concerned, every householder has a clear and inescapable duty of care." The other members of the Tribunal made that *Hear! Hear!* noise, and I'm bound to say I thought the Chairman's distinction was pretty reasonable. I decided to spike my tear-jerking harassment story. It wouldn't be sustainable.

The official stood down soon after, and a senior executive from the Environment Protection Agency took the stand. One of those cold, intimidating people with pale eyes and rimless glasses. Thin, colourless lips. He said that the Agency had initiated a general search of the householder's domestic waste, running a 'bag and tag' operation over the statutory period of six weeks. His tone was dispassionate, his voice dry: but the findings he described were disgusting. There were tin cans in the general waste, and in one search they actually found a couple of hundred and twenty watt electric light bulbs – which have of course been illegal for some years now. Another week the searchers found electric batteries buried among the potato peelings.

The members of the Tribunal shook their heads at this, and even the advocate for the defence looked dismayed. I mean, *every*one, every *child*, knows that if you use electric batteries you are required to dispose of them responsibly – every supermarket and every school has a special box for used electric batteries, which are recognised as a hazardous waste stream.

So the E.P.A executive took the view that the accused was a serial offender. Under an open magistrate's warrant (renewed each year, I gather) an Agency team entered the property of the accused. I expect they would have done this at dawn, smacking the door off its hinges with a manual battering ram – 'The Big Key', as they say in the movies. The occupier, for there was only one, was removed from the premises and taken into secure accommodation.

Within the house, there were endless anomalies and problems. I did not try to note them all, but it seems the roof insulation fell far short of the statutory minimum thickness. Compounding this, the thermostat settings were nowhere near the permitted settings for the time of the year. Predictably, the boiler was out of date, and emitting a dangerously high level of effluent. Worst of all, although there was apparently only this one person living in the house, it had four or more rooms, depending on how you define them. Certainly more than are needed, or indeed nowadays allowed, by standard domestic housing protocols.

This naturally led on to a report from the Medical expert, who was asked if there was anything in the householder's medical condition to explain – it could hardly excuse – this behaviour. She thought not. The advocate for the accused asked if the doctor had personally examined her client, and was told that no examination was necessary. He was not an immigrant, so his medical record was complete and up to date. It was entirely consistent with the E.P.A. report. The accused had a history of obesity-related issues and had agreed to accept medication, but had not attempted to follow the accompanying dietary and exercise regimes.

The Chairman again provided a footnote to the medical evidence: "The Tribunal wished to observe that when competent medical authorities prescribe a course of diet or exercise, it is not a suggestion which the patient may follow or not at their own good pleasure. A medical prescription has the status of an order."

Do you know, I found myself warming to the chairman? Cold and pedantic he might seem, but there was no arguing with his view that what was at issue was not so much the energy wasted in dealing with careless recycling, but what this revealed about the parasitical *attitude* of the householder. It was at the end of the hearing that he said (my shorthand isn't all that brilliant) something like: "Clearly there is no likelihood of any significant improvement in behaviour if we send the accused for counselling or reform. It is a matter of regret that the more robust forms of electro-therapy are forbidden by European Law."

The other members of the tribunal were nodding agreement. "This is not a case of accidental non-compliance with the law. What we have here is deliberate environmental sabotage by a serial offender who rejects the rules and values of our community. We are left with no realistic alternative but to recycle the offender. Subject always to confirmation by Higher Authority, Tribunal therefore finds that this should be done in consultation with the medical authorities, but without delay, so that net social benefit can be maximized. Under statutory regulations, the donor's heart, lungs, kidneys, pancreas and thymus can all be harvested, along with the usual corneas, blood and plasma. Should other physical materials prove to be

24

of medical interest or value, we shall look sympathetically on a request."

So a deviant was going to get his just deserts, making the environment safer and more sustainable for the rest of us. Evidently I had my story! No, better than that – I had a Feature! It would serve to show how vigilantly the E.P.A. works to protect us, and it would illustrate the need for us all to be on our guard against those who would subvert the efforts and sacrifices that we all have to make. Get a quote and photo from the Chairman. The moral could go in italics: *Recycle – or Be Recycled!* I would have my own by-line on this one!

Then the Trade Union woman leaned over to the Chairman, whispering something. The Chairman leaned down to the Clerk of the Court. More whispering. Then the Tribunal members looked across at me, sitting alone in the press box. It was unnerving, like one of those dreams where you are naked in the middle of town.

The Chairman cleared his throat and looked straight at me over his spectacles: "As I remarked when this hearing opened, there is a standing advisory request under DA-Notice 07 (Environmental Agency) that editors and publishers regard the proceedings and findings of this Tribunal as subject to a voluntary press embargo. We trust that it will be fully complied with."

So I didn't have a feature. Even if I wrote it up and took it to the editor, he would be obliged to kill it.

I rose, half-bowed my surrender to the Chairman, and went out into the street. Sure enough, it was still raining. As I turned the collar of my coat up, I saw a couple of Greenshirts helping an elderly woman across the road. The girl marched into the road, raised her hand, and brought the traffic to a halt. Her partner took the woman's elbow gently and guided her off the pavement. I took up position on the other side of the old woman's walking frame, not wanting to get done for jaywalking. "Nasty spot of rain," I remarked, as we slowly crossed over.

"No, sir," the lad said, very earnestly, "it is clean, unpolluted rain. Not like the rain they had in the old days. You know it destroyed whole forests, poisoned our fish and damaged historic buildings?"

It must have been from a lesson he had learned. Acid rain hasn't been a big news item for years now. The cleanup is ongoing, though. Then I thought, maybe I could work up a piece on that. It might not be a candidate for the Pulitzer, but perhaps we have always to remind ourselves that where the environment is concerned, there is no longer any room for passengers – we are all crew.

EZEKIEL

Stuart Wardrop

The compound shimmered in the blistering early afternoon heat. I stared through the grimy glass and felt sweat prickling my brow despite the air con. I had wondered how it would feel being back – and now I knew. The fly-blown patch of dirty sand was every bit as depressing as I remembered and I wondered what had possessed me to return to this God forsaken apology for a country.

I turned as the door opened. Pieter Niessen, *Chef de Mission,* was originally from Utrecht but a lifetime with the UN had turned him into a sort of international citizen.

"Got everything Phil?"

"Yep – all packed and ready." I waved a hand at the compound where two white Toyota pick-ups sat, engines idling to keep the interiors bearable. Each bore the UN logo and in the back of the second one two Burani so-called peacekeepers were doing what they did best – sleeping. "I'm just short of an interpreter, Piet."

"Not any more, my friend. I have the very person." He stood aside and beckoned a second man into the room. "This is Ezekiel. Zeke, meet Phil Armitage, Head Office troubleshooter. He's been here before but that was what – about twelve years ago?" I nodded. "You'll be taking him up country to the Zimburu water project. Zeke nodded and I went to shake his hand. Then I saw that in place of his right hand he wore a hook. He extended his other hand and as I took it I registered with a jolt that not only was his right hand missing but his left leg ended at the knee, replaced by an old-fashioned Long-John-Silver-type peg leg.

Suddenly Piet was speaking. "Zeke's from the mission at Gitego. He's fluent in English and French – the mission saw to that. He also has Swahili and most of the local dialects." He grinned and said drily. "Useful with officialdom." I smiled at the subtext.

I ran my eyes over Zeke and saw a well-built young man dressed in clean and pressed khakis. He seemed about fifteen and wore the closed face and guarded eyes I had seen many times in central Africa. He had fine features, with the long nose and lighter skin of the Ursi but I suspected that like many Barandans he was probably a tribal mixture – perhaps a product of the wholesale rape and savagery that had been my introduction to the country. I knew that anyone recruited by Piet would be mission educated – either a former child soldier or a victim of the Machete Men – or both. I had seen enough of their handiwork when I was last here.

Zeke spoke for the first time. His English was fluent and idiomatic and as if speech had released something in him his impassive face became animated. His smile revealed white, even teeth and his brown eyes met mine directly. "Welcome to Baranda, Mr Armitage. I shall do my best to justify the faith placed in me by Mr Niessen."

"I'm sure you will, Zeke – and call me Phil. If you'd like to put your kit in the truck I think we'd better get on our way before our Burani friends go into a coma." He laughed but his face had momentarily stilled at the word. I looked sharply at him. Useless or not I preferred to keep the Burani onside and I hoped that Zeke had no agenda with them.

. I went to pick up his kit bag but he beat me to it, clamping his hook round the handles and swinging it effortlessly over one shoulder. The Burani stirred, bleary-eyed as we approached. They made no attempt to assist us and settled down again as our little convoy got under way.

Our driver Juma drove sedately out of the compound then was immediately transformed. He hurtled the Toyota through the teeming streets of Dodoma. I hung on white knuckled as we aimed, horn blaring, for impossibly narrow gaps, raced at lunatic speeds towards traffic lights, some of which showed green in both directions and screeched round corners on tortured tyres. On the odd occasion when we slowed down I was conscious of mad-dog stares coming at me from out of the crowd, followed by whistles and jeering catcalls. I looked questioningly at Zeke. He yelled back with a grin. "Don't worry," he yelled, "to them all UN *muzungu* – foreigners – are rich. They might rob you but they don't kill UN people – not nowadays anyway."

I didn't doubt him but was happy nevertheless to leave the capital behind in exchange for a marginally less lunatic progress up the winding, pot-holed road to the Spanish-run water project that had gone hopelessly over budget. The UN was big on water. In the West access to clean water from a tap is considered an inalienable human right and a universal human desire. So why were the locals obstructing this one and why was equipment continually being stolen and sold as scrap? That was what I had been sent from Zurich to find out.

After about an hour of heart in the mouth driving Juma brought the truck to a screeching halt at the project. Once known as Leopoldville this small town had been a favourite vacation resort of the Belgians. Now, having endured successive waves of almost casual savagery at the hands of different warlords Zimburu, as it was now, had turned in on itself. The smell of distrust and fear hung heavy in the sweltering heat of high summer, mingling with a pervasive stench, the origins of which I tried not to think about.

The Burani vanished silently into the peacekeepers' compound, Zeke's eyes trailing them carefully. I was anxious to get cracking and commenced discussions with the Spanish water engineers. The town wasn't the problem. It was the surrounding villages. Each was run by a council of elders and so far they had resisted all attempts by the Spanish to even talk about the project, far less assist with it.

Not having the language I followed my instincts and gave Zeke his head to see where it would lead. I was never sure that he always translated accurately but the villagers laughed a lot, accepted our gifts and offered hospitality by way of vast amounts of powerful maize beer.

It did lead to one spectacular success. The villagers had flatly refused to have a standpipe outside every hut and had angrily ripped out the pipes. After many patient hours of negotiating in the blistering sun – the Barandans seemed impervious to the searing heat – Zeke finally got all the villages to accept a row of standpipes beside the foul and mosquito infested river that served the villagers as joint water supply and sewage disposal.

My time in country was almost up so I settled for this – as I knew my bosses would. The UN is nothing if not pragmatic. As Zeke and I and the Spanish project engineer, Luis Ortez, relaxed with a beer on the night before our return to the capital I asked Zeke how he had done it. He gave me one of the huge beams that lit up his face like a searchlight. "The first thing, Phil, is that these people," he gestured, "are Ursi – like myself. And," to Luis, "the district administrator gave you a Tuhu interpreter." His face stilled at the word but then he grinned. "The two do not mix – have not done so from the beginning of time. Tuhu as well as Burani visited these villages for sport in the war – and afterwards. Did you not see the numbers of...?" He raised his hook and tapped his peg leg.

I nodded. This explained Zeke's attitude to the Burani soldiers and on impulse I said. "Is that how you...?"

"No Phil, this," he raised his hook, "happened in Dodoma – about twelve years ago, just as the war was finishing. Didn't Mr Niessen say that you were here then?"

"Yes – part of the first UN peacekeeping force. I know what it was like in Dodoma." I shivered at the memory.

"Zeke smiled but his eyes were far away. "Yes. That's how I got to the mission you know." My eyebrows asked the question but Luis was impatient to get on. Zeke glanced at him and continued. "Your Tuhu interpreter could have spoken with the elders for all eternity and they would happily have made all the promises you wanted. But these promises would never be kept – partly because he was Tuhu but mainly because stealing to survive has become as natural as breathing in this country."

I registered Luis's frown. "What about the standpipes, Zeke? How did you swing that?"

"They're different." Zeke grinned. "For a white *muzungu,* this makes no sense. Why would anyone fetch filthy water by hand when they could have clean water from a tap? What of the women and girls who do the fetching? Would they prefer a tap at the front door?" He laughed. "The answer – and this makes perfect sense to the villagers – is no, they would not. Why? Because for as long as anyone can remember walking through the village to fetch water has been how girls caught the eyes of boys. By putting a pipe outside every hut, Luis, you destroyed their marriage market."

On that note we turned in and the following day, despite Juma's best efforts we arrived safely in the UN compound in the capital. Two different Burani accompanied us this time and again I was conscious of a tenseness about Zeke when they were around.

Back in the air-conditioned comfort of Piet's office I watched my report take shape on the laptop screen. Zeke sat quietly drinking beer from a long-necked bottle.

"Zeke?" He looked up. "I don't know what might come of it but I'm putting in a bit about how helpful you've been. In fact it's more than that. I could never have done it without you." He grinned and took a pull at the bottle. "I need your full name and if you don't mind something about you. There must be thousands of Ezekiels in Africa and I want to be sure they credit the right one."

"OK. My full name is Ezekiel M'kara and I think I am about fifteen years old. What else is there? I don't know much more. The mission people got me from the Danish army hospital. I was very small and very weak and of course," he laughed shortly, "my hand and leg were somewhere else. They thought I would die but I survived and – well – here I am."

"What about your family?"

His face clouded. "No family. They think my family died in the last days of the fighting in Dodoma." I frowned as memory stirred in the furthest reaches of my mind. He went on. "That's why I have my name," he smiled. "The mission gives children biblical first names and they had reached the letter E in the alphabet. So I became Ezekiel – Zeke. My family name was an obvious problem so they gave me the name of the soldier who took me to the hospital and I made it look Barandan." He shrugged. "And now you know as much about me as I do. Any more beer?"

I wasn't listening. I was staring hard at the name on the screen. Ezekiel M'kara. M'kara… Macara, M'kara… Macara. Christ, it couldn't be. I smelled again the stomach-turning stench from the alley as a face swam into my mind, pale under the tan and the day old bristles. "Boss, you'd better see this. We've got a live one – sort of." I signalled to Weaver to take over and entered the dark mouth of the alley. It was hot and silent except for the sluggish buzzing of the flies and the dry retching of trooper Foy. As we approached a pile of rags the stink made me gag and I recognised the unmistakable coppery smell of blood.

I could still see that alleyway and the bloody rags that had gradually resolved into a scattered heap of arms, legs, heads and torsos. I recalled registering a new horror. None of these body parts was attached to anything. My stomach contracted and it was only by an enormous effort of will that I avoided adding to the fetid mess. I felt a hand on my arm. "Boss?" I nodded and the sergeant led me to one side of the pile. There on the ground lay a small shape, shiny with dried blood and dominated by an enormous pair of eyes. Then with a sharp intake of breath I realised why this child's body was small. It was minus a leg and a hand.

"Get him out of here. The Danish field hospital's closest. Then double back here. We've got Machete Men to chase."

"Right boss," said Sergeant Macara.

Zeke was speaking again. I wrenched my thoughts back to the present. He was looking at me anxiously. "Are you alright, Phil? You seem a bit er… distant."

"Yes I'm fine, Zeke. Someone walking over my grave, that's all." I was debating what to do next when he spoke again.

"Do you need me any more, Phil? I really have to get back to the mission house. I've been away long enough."

"What about the future then?" I said, stalling for time.

He hesitated then appeared to make up his mind. "Phil, remember the maize beer?"

"Yes."

Where d'you think it came from?"

"Maize, I suppose." I laughed uncertainly.

Zeke's voice became clipped and businesslike. "Tell me. Did you see any maize growing up there?" I shook my head and he went on. "You saw women, old men and cripples like me. All the young men – the ones the Machete Men left – are slaving for starvation wages in the mines in the north and the bush has taken the maize fields back."

"Can't the women…?"

"Why? When all they need is sitting in the UN warehouse? It's grown in East Africa and shipped here as UN aid."

I made to speak but he waved me into silence. "My country is drowning in handouts, poverty and corruption. We must stand on our own two feet – if enough of us are left with two feet." He laughed abruptly, then his face closed down and the words came softly but with chilling intensity. "There is no future until," he fixed me with his gaze, "the curse of the Burani and the Tuhu has been excised from my country forever – and in the only way they understand." He tapped his leg with his hook.

ANCIENTS

Helen Taylor

"Why did the Ancients become extinct?"

How often as a child had Cassie 12497 asked that question, carefully enunciating the last word, so her crèche-mates couldn't snigger and chant, "Ancients stink! Ancients stink!"

She had always been fascinated by those long ago people, who lived without the security of the Domes, open to all the weather conditions the planet could throw at them – and the children, raised by their gene providers in 'families' – surely a waste of hard-won resources, not to mention a source of favouritism and strife. And now she might be able to come up with an answer to the mystery that had intrigued her since her youth. She stood on this, the first excavation that she had led since qualifying as an archaeologist, and viewed the contours of the land. The workers had retired back to camp as the afternoon cooled into evening to recharge their batteries, but she couldn't resist the opportunity to survey the site by herself.

She made her way to the first trench. This had exposed a stretch of ancient roadway: it was an amazing construction, hard-wearing and practically indestructible. Easy to excavate too. She tried to envisage how it would have looked all those long years ago, filled with cars, lorries or (her own personal favourite) motorcycles. On their way to who knew where…

Maybe on their way to one of the great religious centres of the world, the Disneys. It would seem the cult of Disney had permeated almost the whole world in the olden days. Some only attended the cinemas to see movies celebrating the heroes of Disney. But those luckier, richer or more fanatical were able to travel on pilgrimage to the 'lands', maybe wearing the cult costumes and riding curious-looking cars as part of the worship. Some archaeologists disputed the results of the excavation of the 'land' far to the north but Cassie couldn't come up with any better explanation.

It must have been amazing to be able to travel so easily. Cassie envied the ancients their freedom though in all honesty she had been surprised at how easily she had been granted permission to travel and how much she had been assisted to organize the expedition. The only piece of red tape had been that, as she was on her own, with only robot workers to help her, she had been allocated an official, Smith 9645, whom she had to video-call every evening. It was an indication of her isolation that she looked forward to this contact, even if it was with a relative stranger. She had grown more reliant than she'd ever thought likely on the grey-haired, grey-faced bureaucrat with his flat voice and watchful eyes.

She moved over nearer to the area that had produced a handful of coins and metal cutlery. From this and other material evidence, the site appeared to be the remains of a restaurant or café, as they were called. There was the frontage, once filled with tables, chairs and covered with a canopy and the interior, shadier and cooler. She was slightly sceptical about what she had read: that here people could eat however much they liked whenever they liked. How on earth, with one part of the planet starving and the other part obese, had they thought that a good idea? So much better to collect all the food and water to allocate it fairly. She felt in her back pocket for the foil-wrapped ration bar she had tucked there for lunch.

And yet, she imagined the table and chairs and the awning, bright in the sunlight, the diners clinking glasses and enjoying chatting relaxedly over a bottle of wine. Had she a time machine, she would visit this very restaurant back in the old days and sample a day of ordinary – to her extraordinary – life.

She made her way to the salt pan that in the Silicon Age had been a sea. Apparently holiday makers had come to this city to bathe in the salt water and the sun. Hardly imaginable now: the heat was so intense, the perspiration trickled over her tinted goggles despite the protective suit she wore to deflect the rays. She couldn't understand why, while sunbathing was one of the things – like smoking, alcohol, drugs and travel – that harmed their health, the ancients never gave it up. Madness!

Still shaking her head indulgently at the paradox, Cassie knelt to examine a patch of darker soil. She was so accustomed to living beneath the protective domes that it felt odd to be outdoors. At first, whenever the wind blew, she imagined a storm rising. In fact, she had initially wondered if she would be able to cope. However she was getting more used to it now, less anxious – and just as well. Her travel plans were set in stone: she and her equipment would be picked up two months hence, before the hurricane season truly arrived, by the same vast helicopter that had brought her.

Actually, now she looked to the south, over the sparkling salt flats, she could see an area of darkness. All at once, the world seemed uncannily still, no breath of wind, not even the drone of insects or the occasional bird to break the silence. And the darkness was approaching faster and faster.

She spun around and headed back to base as fast as she could. Every few paces, she looked over her shoulder and saw the spinning vortex grow closer as if aimed directly at her. Stumbling as she ran, she realized with a curse that it was gaining on her at such a rate that she would never make it back in time.

All at once, the light grew dimmer and the wind increased and she was being buffeted around, hardly able to see where she was heading through the barrage of rain and grit that infiltrated her suit and smashed her goggles. The wind snatched at her, spinning her round till she lost her footing. She picked herself up and started to run again. But now she had no idea where she was heading, whether towards shelter or directly into the storm and she was falling again, downhill, tumbling and spinning amid a bombardment of rubble and debris that was falling on her, battering her so that she could only curl up and close her eyes, lungs burning, barely breathing... Then, suddenly, miraculously, there were arms about her, tugging at her and carrying her into no less a darkness, but one in which, blessedly, the wind and rain had abated and there was silence...

When Cassie returned to consciousness she lay for a moment, trying to work out where she lay. Before her was a natural stone wall. She traced it with shaking fingers. It was smooth and slick, as if damp. It was dark, but she could hear voices. Quickly she turned round: beyond a stony outcrop she could see figures moving, silhouetted in a strange, almost living light.

She sat up with a start, despite her body's aches, for a clearer view, knocking a cover that had been placed over her. She did not recognise the material from which it was manufactured. She missed its warmth and bent to retrieve it. It was flexible and covered in hair, just like animal skins she had seen in a museum. Looking around her, she thought that she might be in some natural Dome. It was lit with torches of actual flame that danced off spires and pillars of stone, some reaching from the ceiling, some lifting from the floor, others stretching the full span from roof to ground, all reflected in a pool of still water. On the walls were painted animals, seeming to leap and prance in the flickering light, bulls, horses and deer, all relics of an even earlier age.

She could hear subdued voices, but could not recognize the language however hard she tried. She peered at them. They were strangely clad in swathes of white material that would reflect the sunlight, but the erratic light made it hard for her to see more. With a start, she realized that one of these people was sitting

34

close to her, watching her intently, so still and darkly clad that he was barely visible in the shadows of the cavern. The stranger barked something unintelligible at her – though the gesture that accompanied it told her to stay where she was – and strode off towards the light.

Cassie followed him with her eyes, saw him reporting to another, who turned and looked in her direction. She supposed him to be their leader. He was taller than the rest and, spotlit by the torches for a second, she could see him remove the cloth that covered his head and all of his face apart from his eyes. The leader came over. He looked to be the same age as Cassie, but with a more lined face baked brown by sun or weather, the archaeologist supposed. It made his eyes all the bluer in contrast.

"You are well?"

The voice was slow, with a strange inflection, but Cassie could distinguish the words. She nodded, unable to speak. Her throat was too dry and she was, she realised, afraid. The man offered her a drink which she accepted gratefully, without suspicion: had they any enmity towards her, they would have left her to the storm. Despite the strange taste, it spread a glowing warmth throughout her body and made her more relaxed. He then offered her something – food? She nibbled at it. It had a strange, strong flavour but she found she was ravenous and gulped it down.

"I found you in the storm. I could not leave anyone to suffer, maybe die there, even one such as you."

"Thank you… But who are you? Why are you here? I don't understand…"

"We are the Remnant. We live the old way, following the herds. We live a long way off, further North where the weather is cooler and far from your Domes. But every year a group of us comes to the Great Dead Sea for salt. It is dangerous – we travel at night to avoid the eyes of the sun and your people – but it is a vital commodity for us."

"I thought all the survivors went to the Domes. And how is it dangerous for you to travel here? I don't understand!"

"Not everyone wanted to go to the Domes. And your people hunt us down like vermin."

"How? Nobody knows about you. I study the past and no one has ever mentioned…"

"Maybe it is not common knowledge. But your Technocrats certainly know of us. They do not approve of us, our way of life. Our freedom. Our existence proves that one can live outside the Domes they use to control you. It is a hard way of life, but it is possible."

Cassie could only stare at him, dumbfounded.

"The storm has faded now. You should return to your camp. We would prefer that you keep silent about us but really it is no concern of ours if you tell: your leaders already know of us and we leave tomorrow. I don't imagine that you would be able to find us again even if you wanted. Even if a force is sent against us, we know the land better than any of your race. We can evade them easily."

He gestured for Cassie to rise and they made their way into the main cavern. She could see the rest of the group. Some were sullen, but most had fear in their eyes as they turned to watch her. Cassie could see one, younger than the rest, cower against another. There was no doubt about it, she decided, they knew of her people, enough to be afraid or hostile. And yet they did not seem to want to harm her, accepting their leader's decision as final. She felt as if she had stepped back in time to mankind's earliest days. She longed to know more about their lives but was afraid to ask questions in case they thought she was spying on them.

"I will not betray you. I owe you my life."

The words came readily to her lips – too readily perhaps. The leader only smiled.

"Then we wish you well. Come now."

She was led through a maze of twisting tunnels in almost total darkness. The Remnant seemed to know where the cavern system led, while she stumbled along, sandwiched between the leader and another of his tribe. Eventually after what seemed an eternity of pure blackness, she could see the horns of a moon appearing over the lip of the cave and feel the first stirrings of the air. She was then led back towards her camp in a light that would previously have seemed too slight to guide her, but now seemed ample. As soon as she recognized her surroundings, she touched the leader's arm.

"I know where I am now. Thank you and farewell."

He nodded solemnly in reply and he and his companion disappeared into the night, as silent as ever.

Once ensconced in the comfort of her caravan, Cassie stretched out, then saw a light flashing. Smith had obviously attempted to call her. She was lost in thought for a long while, pondering the ease with which she had received approval and assistance with her project, the equipment and robots allocated readily. Almost reluctantly, she pressed the call back button. The screen flickered into life and Smith's austere face appeared, mouth pinched and a worry frown evident.

"Where have you been? I called a number of times, but you did not reply.

The robots are back in their berth. Due to a storm, they reported."

So she was being more closely monitored than she had supposed.

"Yes. I was caught up in it. I'd gone out at midday, while they were recharging and it swept up to me. I've never seen anything move so quickly. It was… terrifying."

"What did you do?"

"I got lost when it caught up with me. I managed to find a sort of shelter in some rocks and then made my way back to base."

Smith's eyes narrowed, "It took you some time to return. The storm blew itself out hours ago."

She could feel a degree of panic building up.

"I was lost. It took me a while to find my bearings again. The storm was so powerful… If you'd ever been caught in one, you'd understand."

Smith shuddered theatrically, "Bless the Domes that protect us."

He paused, then added, "I don't suppose you've noticed anything strange in the vicinity?"

His tones were neutral, almost casual, but Cassie could see attention in his eyes.

"Not sure I understand. Nothing strange. Apart from the storm, that is."

"Very well."

The screen went dead. Cassie thought it odd that he had not given her a time to report the next day. She sat back, exhausted. She hadn't wanted to lie, but how could she endanger the very people who had saved her from the storm. Now, though, she knew that her suspicions were accurate: she had been planted here – as bait? As a spy? She wasn't sure, but everything was making sense now. And she also knew the answer to her childhood question: the Ancients were not extinct. Now, though, she would have to decide what she should do with that knowledge.

Just then, there was a crescendo of noise and she leapt to her feet. It was the sound of an approaching helicopter. They must have been waiting nearby to monitor her activity. How much did they know? Cassie strode over to the door to face the coming storm.

LUING

Roderick Manson

For Irene Malchaski

A flying carpet
carved
from the memory of rust
corrodes me across
the eroding flow
to Luing.

Luing,
the signage pensively proclaims,
is
"A place to think –
A place to be".

Well,
isn't that true
of everywhere?
Unkind to the ferry
my words
may have been
but a deeper corrosion
is in these words
that scamper away
from meaning
from fear
of what that meaning
might reveal.

Today
I find it
a place to think
of being wet
and a place
to be –
wet

as the asphalt-tortured snake,
its sole remaining fang
fossilised
in a whitewashed trig point in the north;
its trig point rattle
in the distant south
a remnant of that time
when Scotland
was American
and Europe
and England
just a tale
to frighten children
who might some day
come to pass
and live here.

Or wet
as the bracken hillside,
scythed by Autumn tempests
like Campbells
at Inverlochy
beneath the Highland maelstrom
of MacDonald
and Montrose.

Or wet
as birch-capillaries
pulsing elixir
to the moss-green slopes
to feed the seeds
on that flesh
of leaves
passed
in the inevitable winds.

Here,
as anywhere,
all flesh is not grass
but it is,
very largely,
water
and
in this
it mirrors me.

But,
between the deluge
and the merely mist
that hangs
like flypaper
to catch what fate
may send
there is that western haze,
half-glimpsed
in the blue
of sea
and the green
of Luing
so far from the grey
of my life.

TAY BEAVERS

Roderick Manson

All across this wasted land
are legends
where a hero did to death
the last wolf.

There are no tales
of where you slew
the last beaver
but nevertheless we're back

outside your law,
bubbly,
brown
and bushy-tailed
and when,
this time,
you come for us
remember this

we bite.

MOVING ON

Cathy Whitfield

To begin with Joe didn't pay much attention to the rain. It wasn't as if he could go outside and, in any case, rain suited his mood. He wasn't sleeping well and the hiss on the roof, the scutter of showers rattling against the window-panes and the rush of water in the drain that ran alongside the track were soothing sounds that kept the dreams at a distance.

The dreams had been bad since the accident, especially the ones where he watched his ice-axe bite into a spongy layer of ice gone rotten in an unseasonably mild winter and felt himself falling. Usually he woke before the impact but sometimes, in the dream, the rock smashed into his spine and he'd sit up, confused, not knowing where he was, or what.

Every day that summer, his first in the Mill House, had brought rain in one form or another. Sometimes it would arrive out of an empty sky, without sound or shape, a blurring of the light that thickened imperceptibly so that it wasn't until Joe heard the hiss of static that he'd realise it was raining. At other times it was a thunderous deluge out of a slate-coloured sky, or a weeping mizzle that shrouded the house in an ashen gloom. But, whatever its form, it was always grey

His friends and family thought he was mad, moving to the Fens. "It's miles from anywhere!" By which they meant miles from them. But to Joe that was the whole point of leaving London as soon as his rehabilitation was deemed to be complete.

"How are you going to manage on your own?" they'd wanted to know. *The way you are now.* They hadn't said it though. Joe had learned to be grateful for certain silences.

"Technology," he'd replied a little too brightly. "I'll have the internet, and phones do actually work there you know." He'd order everything he needed online and get it delivered. He promised to keep in touch by Skype and e-mail but hadn't. He'd become too familiar with all the forms of pity – the friends who, not knowing what to say, said nothing at all and, worse, the ones who, with hopeless optimism, declared that he'd soon be back on his feet, although everyone knew he wouldn't be. He'd even found Jennifer's steadfast practicality to be unbearable.

"You have to accept your limitations, Joe, and move on." Which he'd felt to be an insensitive choice of words.

"I can't move anywhere. In case you hadn't noticed I'm a …" He'd faltered at this, the most minor of hurdles.

"Say it," she'd insisted and so, with an effort that made him want to weep, he had.

"I'm a paraplegic – a fucking cripple! I can't go anywhere or do anything!"

"You can if you try. I'm here Joe. But you'll have to walk towards me."

He'd sworn at her with uncharacteristic savagery, pouring out all his frustrations and anger in a torrent of vitriol.

"I'm still here," she'd said quietly when he'd finished, then turned on her heel and walked away. He'd never forgive her for that – not for walking away, since it was the best thing she could have done for herself – but for having the power to walk away when he had no power at all.

So it was hardly surprising that he'd fled – in as much as a man who's lost the use of his legs can flee – to the house he bought in the Fens with the insurance money, a house he'd never even seen. All he'd wanted was a refuge from the past he longed for and the future he couldn't face. The landscape of the Fens was part of the refuge, its flat distances and vast skies so utterly different from the mountains, and he'd chosen the house for its outlook to a relentless horizon where water and sky merged, each reflecting the other. The Fens were permeated with marshes and meres, streams and rivers, a reclaimed land whose dikes and culverts barely contained all that water. The house itself had once been part of the land's battle but the watermill was long gone, leaving behind only its name and the millpond at the far end of the garden.

It was a place unlike any he'd ever known, a place where he believed he could work. Black Diamond had sent him a couple of ice-axes to review, which he considered tactless, but maybe they didn't know what had happened. The axes lay on a sofa in the living room. He couldn't even bear to touch them. *Rock and Ice* had asked him to write an article on ice-climbs in the Rjukan Valley. Since that was where he'd fallen, he thought that tactless too. But, worse of all, Harper Collins wanted him to write his memoirs. He was only thirty-two. Surely you don't write your memoirs until your life's almost over? But then it was.

He needed the money though, so he had to accept, but he'd done no work at all since coming to the Fens and had just wheeled himself from room to room, staring out of the windows, watching the rain fall and the water rise. He could almost feel the land grow spongy, the leaden sky squeezing the moisture back out of the ground so that the fields become pocked with pools. The millpond swelled and overflowed so that the drain beside the track to the house turned into a stream. He supposed this happened often and wasn't alarmed, but the man who delivered his groceries took a more pessimistic view.

"It's that there global warming," he said dolefully. "Wasn't like this when I was a boy and I've lived here all my life. Seen it coming, I have – wetter summers and the floods worse year on year. Get your house cheap, did you? I'm not surprised. Folks around here are all moving away. Talk about a ghost town – this is a ghost country." He jerked his head at the road that led towards the etched blur of the nearest town. "See that road? It'll be under water before long, you mark my words. Best move out while you can. This is no place for a –" He stopped abruptly, his face reddening.

"Quite," Joe said dryly, but didn't take the man's advice. There was no way he was crawling back to London, literally or otherwise. But it kept on raining and, true to the man's prediction, the road did indeed flood, but he still wasn't concerned. He'd stocked up with food and fuel – enough to see him through until the water went down again and the road opened. He even felt a reluctant admiration for the rain which was causing the flooding. Up until then he'd considered rain to be quixotic and ephemeral, but now it had changed its character, changed the rules. It was as if rain had declared war on the land, allied itself with the rivers and streams who were marching inland like some vast invading army whose onslaught nothing and no one could withstand. There was a magnificent inevitability about it all.

It wasn't until the electricity went off that he realised things were serious, that he was too dependent on technology, too dependent on power. He still had batteries for essential equipment – his laptop, radio, torches, the motor on his chair – but as the rain kept falling and the water went on rising, the electricity remained off and, one by one, his batteries gave up the ghost. Even the radio's increasingly alarming weather reports eventually gave way to a dull hiss barely distinguishable from the hiss of the rain outside.

His phone still had power, however, and after several attempts he got through to a harassed woman at the Environment Agency who assured him that rescue was on its way. "Just stay in the house," she recommended, a piece of advice which made him smile wryly. Like he had any choice.

He should never have come to the Fens. Everyone had been right. He'd done no research, hadn't appreciated the risks. He should have understood how marginal his life was and never come to a place that was equally marginal. The world was changing. He'd seen that to his cost. The climate was taking the land back, taking livelihoods with it, and no-one had the power to stop it. He found it oddly comforting to know he wasn't alone in feeling powerless.

It was the next day, around dawn, when the rain came in for the kill. He heard a growl of triumph, as if a besieging army had broken through the defences of a citadel. He wheeled himself to the French windows in time to see a wave of water, shot through with fence-posts, come charging towards him. Some dyke must have been breached, he understood vaguely, as the water burst though the French doors. He grabbed a radiator as the water surged into the room, swung his chair to one side and swirled about the room in a grey slurry of silt and branches, rising first to his ankles, then his knees. It wasn't until it reached his waist that he remembered the phone in his top pocket and, still clinging to the radiator, dialled 999.

"Can you get upstairs?" a woman asked. She sounded just as harassed as the one from the Environment Agency when he explained that he didn't have an upstairs. "Then can you manage to get onto the roof?"

For a moment he wanted to laugh. The roof, a mere ten feet above him, was as remote as the moon.

"I'm –" he began.

Say it. He seemed to hear Jennifer's voice even above the clamour of the water. *Say it!*

"I'm sure I'll manage…"

You idiot! he thought. Why couldn't he have said he was in a wheelchair, that he was a paraplegic, that he needed help? That the water was still rising and he was powerless to stop it? *You have to accept your limitations,* Jennifer had said. *Accept them and die,* he thought, imagining the headline. 'Crippled Rock-Jock drowned in Fens Floods'.

Accept your limitations, Joe. Accept what he could no longer do. Why was it necessary for him to be clinging to a radiator in imminent risk of drowning before he could understand what she'd really meant – that he needed to find out not what he couldn't do, but what he could.

So he let go of the radiator.

The force of the water swung him sideways, toppling the chair, dragging him under the surface. He tried to kick up with his legs and when, inevitably, he failed, flailed out with his arms instead and grabbed the sofa to haul himself up. The Black Diamond ice axes were still there. He gripped one of them, slammed it into the back of the sofa to stop himself from sliding back into the water and hooked the other around the sofa's arm. Slowly, using the axes, hooking himself to anything he could reach, he pulled himself and his useless legs towards the shattered door and out into the swirling waters. Then he let go.

The house had been built in the mid-eighteen hundreds and had never been looked after. The estate agent had recommended repointing but Joe had never got around to arranging it – an oversight that might be about to save his life. The force of the water slammed him against the kitchen wall, and he hooked one ice axe to the window-sill to hold himself in place. Looking up, he could see that the uneven crumbling wall was less than a pitch in height, not anything like as far as the moon. He slammed his right-hand axe up into the wall, felt it dig into the mortar and hook on brick, then pulled up and drove the tip of the left-hand axe higher up the wall. And again and again until he was free of the water. Only then did he look down and, conscious of the weight of his legs dragging at his body, feel a moment of doubt. But hadn't he conquered the overhanging section of the Helmcken Falls, hanging at times from one hand?

He looked back up the wall and began to think like a climber, planning each move, searching out the tiny ledges that would give him purchase, assessing the weakness of the guttering and, hanging from one axe, smashing it with the other so that he could get a grip on the tarred and felted flat roof of the kitchen. Getting over the edge was the crux of this particular climb but, with an effort that made him want to weep, he pulled himself up and over until he was safe, spread-eagled on the roof. Eventually he eased himself up onto one elbow to take stock of his situation.

He was on an island a few feet above a swirling tide of glinting grey water. In the distance, on the horizon, he could make out a church tower, but where there had once been fields there was nothing now but a huge lake, punctuated by the scribbled outlines of trees and, here and there, the roofs of farm buildings. The sun, still rising, slid between two bars of pewter cloud and spread itself across the water like mercury, turning the matt grey flood into a shivering sheet of silver and steel. Now he could truly appreciate the extent of the flooding and the power of the water, and realise how small he was. But not powerless. Limited, perhaps, but there's always something that can be done. Everything can be adapted to.

The sun was higher now. It had even stopped raining. Joe caught sight of something yellow moving towards him, the colour joyfully vivid against the grey of water and sky – an inflatable powering towards him. He considered phoning the emergency woman again to let her know he was on the roof. He punched in the number but it wasn't the emergency services who answered because that wasn't who he'd called.

"Jen?" he said. "It's me. Are you still there…?"

HOT AIR

Ann Prescott

"Do I have to spell it out, Maggie? Get up there!"

"I hear and obey. I'm to go to this Kinross place, find out what they are doing, and tell them to stop."

"Just do it!"

The furious face of the PM disappeared and the wall screen blanked.

Magenta Hart, Minister of Power and Supply, swore under her breath and surveyed her team who were gathered for the usual Monday morning briefing. Her Chief Science Advisor, her PA, her PA's assistant, and the Media Secretary simulated complete absorption in tasks that demanded their full attention. Only the Downing Street cat, a ginger tom half the size of his ego, met her gaze with wide, unblinking eyes.

She already had enough on her hands preparing for next month's negotiations on the Energy Quotas. Although it was fifty odd years ago that Russia cut the pipes, the psyches of many of her European counterparts bore the scars from the ensuing two decades of gas riots. Yet she was being sent, correction, *ordered* on this wild goose chase because some god-forsaken TV station in the back of beyond happened to mention methane. What was wrong with video linking all of a sudden? There hadn't been a whiff of anything untoward during the weekend with Freddie at Chequers. Nevertheless here he was, barely two hours after she'd left him, getting his Ys in a twist – over what precisely?

Forty-eight hours later Magenta Hart was approaching the grey stone building that proclaimed itself as the Centre of Human Resilience. She'd come up on the overnight, pampering herself with a hot shower and breakfast in Edinburgh. She took a final glance at her briefing note. At the top of the sheet, underneath the date, was the legend 'Burns Night'. For a split second she panicked. Was there some special greeting, 'Hoots', perhaps? She felt many miles from her comfort zone in this country of frosted fields and sugar-mice hills. Hadn't her father mentioned holidays in Scotland? That must have been long before the imposition of travel restrictions. The driver held open the car door. Someone had brushed a path through the snow. Two fabric 'trees' flanked the entrance and, as she recognised these iconic structures, the information she had been given about Kinross Electrics made sense for the first time. This was the company who manufactured the ubiquitous MFC – microbial fuel cell – assemblies that were supposed to convert grey water into clean water and generate electricity in the process.

A youngish woman emerged from the building. She wore tunic and trousers, a tad monochrome, crisp and business-like but definitely not on trend; nice shoes though. Maggie wouldn't mind being seen in them herself. Maggie swung her elegant, purple clad legs out of the car, tossed her shoulder length red-gold hair, arranged her famous pussy-cat smile, and seized the initiative.

"You must be Dr Jackson? I'm Magenta Hart."

The woman smiled back, meeting her green eyes head on with her own grey ones. "Good Morning Minister. Yes, I'm Anna Jackson. Welcome to Kinross. Come inside out of the cold and I'll let you know what we have planned – all subject to your approval of course. First of all I must apologise for that appalling media leak. Although I knew nothing about it at the time I do hold myself responsible."

Maggie hadn't anticipated such an admission. With unfailing instinct she recognised that the only time to kick someone is when she's down.

"The Prime Minister is very concerned that our European neighbours might be alarmed at the fact that a company in the UK is apparently manufacturing methane. I hope that I will be able to assure him that that is far from the truth."

Dr Jackson didn't reply directly. Instead she led her into a high room with a number of oversized onion shapes in the centre.

"We thought it would be helpful if I started with the model of the AD plant, Minister."

"I have no wish to be bombarded with a lot of techno-babble."

"Bear with me a moment. Legislation makes it compulsory to dispose of specified bio-waste, such as food, in the anaerobic digester."

Magenta Hart tapped her foot.

"The technology is old as the hills of course, and well understood," Dr Jackson added quickly before she could be interrupted again. "The products are digestate, which is marketed as a fertiliser and soil improver, and mobane which fuels our public transport."

"Dr Jackson, so far you have not told me anything with which I'm not already familiar."

"Perhaps you are not aware that mobane is the trade name for compressed methane."

"You're telling me mobane and methane are the same?" Maggie exclaimed, temporarily loosing her cool.

"Yes, Minister. The biogas from the digester – that's this big dome – contains around 20–30% impurities, mainly carbon dioxide and some sulfides that are scrubbed here." She indicated another part of the model. "The gas that is left is, to all intents and purpose, pure methane."

"Are Kinross Electrics licensed for this?" was the incredulous response.

"Lots of companies market mobane, often under different names, but the fuel that drives public road transport in the UK and on the continent of Europe is definitely compressed methane."

The face of her Scientific Advisor crawled into Maggie's consciousness. The rat, she thought. I'll have his balls in a bag for this. He'll have buried the facts under those reams about –ase this and –ase that, when one sentence could have stopped me making a fool of myself. Of all the underhand…

"Do you mind if I consult my Chief Scientific Advisor?" she asked sweetly. "If your company is already manufacturing methane legitimately I should like to hear from him precisely where he feels the problem lies."

"I'll rustle up some coffee, or would you prefer tea?"

"Tea with lemon would be lovely."

Rat-face was standing by as pre-arranged but the ensuing scribe was most unsatisfactory and apart from confirming that mobane and methane were indeed the same, did nothing to enlighten her. She was becoming more and more convinced there was chicanery afoot. So what if she didn't have a science background? His job was to enlighten her not to land her in the shit. Why had Freddie been so keen to get her out of London? It would be like him to toss her to the wolves if Rat-face had persuaded him a cabinet re-shuffle was politically advantageous. Opportunity or threat? That Jackson woman could be an ally, albeit an unwitting one. She approved of her confident bearing, her straightforward manner of speech, and her shoes.

That Jackson woman returned bearing tea and a plate of shortbread biscuits. "I have a message from the CEO asking whether you would like to sample haggis and neeps for lunch. Don't feel you have to. It's traditional fare for Burns Night. Besides it gives our production manager his annual opportunity to blow his own bagpipes."

The Minister purred, "Do call me Maggie, Anna." She leaned forward slightly. "Yes, I certainly would. Please thank him; it sounds fun. We read some of Burns' poems at school but they lost a lot in the pronunciation! Was he born in Kinross?"

"No, our claim to fame is Mary, Queen of Scots, She was imprisoned on an island in Loch Leven – that's the stretch of water on your right as you came in – you can row across the water to view the ruins of the castle."

"How romantic! And how my daughter would love that. I must remember to tell her. I'm afraid I don't see nearly enough of her. She lives in Hampshire with my partner. Do you have children, Anna?"

As Anna replied Maggie spared a thought for her daughter. Maybe she should make the effort to see the girl – and Bill. She wondered if he'd taken up with anyone yet or was doggedly faithful as always. Her long nails curled round her cup. Anna was still speaking. Apparently she had only been back at work a couple of months having taken a year out following the birth of her baby daughter. Her son was a few years older. Her husband was a development scientist at KE.

Maggie re-focussed the conversation. "Which brings me back to the vexed question of methane."

"I can fill you in with the background if you are prepared to listen. Let me know when I descend into techno-babble. "

"You're on," said Maggie, mentally ceding one point to Anna.

"We'll start with the basics. Do you understand the relationship between carbon dioxide and methane?"

"To be perfectly frank I haven't the foggiest. Knowledge of chemistry isn't obligatory for the job and, speaking personally, I abandoned the subject with a glad heart while the sap was still rising. I know carbon dioxide is the notorious greenhouse gas and its formula C-O-2 if that helps."

"Well, methane is C-H-4."

"Like H-2-0."

Anna looked puzzled for a moment, and then she smiled. "I see. 2 Hs for every O you mean. Fine. They are like two sides of a coin. Carbon dioxide can't be changed chemically into methane but, when methane is burned in air, it reacts with oxygen and turns into carbon dioxide and water, swaps two Os for four Hs if you like."

"And the carbon dioxide floats away and becomes greenhouse gas?"

"That's the downside. The benefit is the huge quantity of energy that is released by the reaction. For example, in an internal combustion engine, the energy from mobane is converted into the mechanical energy that drives the buses. The Elizabethans used the energy to generate electricity in gas-fired power stations. I believe that, in olden days, quite ordinary people actually had methane gas piped into their homes for heating and cooking."

"Before Russia cut the pipes I take it! I think I'm beginning to get the scenario. Burning methane indiscriminately creates quantities of carbon dioxide and carbon dioxide is a green house gas; hence the PM's anxiety."

"He'd be justified if that was all there was to it. You'll have heard of Sir Paul Melville and his work on MFCs?" Anna took Maggie's nod as affirmation. "He's our local celebrity. He's active in the company although he must be well in his eighties. You'll meet him at lunch. His career is a something of a fairy tale. He's supposed to have discovered the strain of geoactive bacteria used in KE's MFCs when he was researching bioremediation at the University of North Tay. Then, when he joined KE himself, he initiated the ground-breaking work on electrodes, making use of the know-how gained last century in the manufacture of polypropylene in Dundee and Fife.

"I noticed the 'trees' at the entrance. They looked a tad old-fashioned."

"They were the first two off the production line. That unfortunate media leak related to Sir Paul's most recent innovation. It really is ground-breaking. By modifying MFC technology, the KE scientists can transform carbon dioxide back into methane."

Maggie pounced. She could hardly believe her luck.

"You mean re-cycle the greenhouse gas?

"Precisely."

"Who knows about this?"

"The Tay Television broadcast only mentioned a process for manufacturing methane so I suppose you are the first, apart from senior company personnel of course. The plant is only at the development stage. It will be eighteen months at least before the process goes commercial. Then there would be the business of getting it approved."

"What would be the market? More public transport?"

"The CEO suggested calling it 'thermane' and selling it, under licence needless to say, as fuel for heating industrial premises, public buildings and so forth, maybe for cooking in restaurants."

Maggie could have danced on her tippy-toes. Had Rat-face and his gang known what was going on? Highly unlikely! And Freddie could knit himself into knots if he wanted. Minister announces plans to recycle greenhouse gas! Carbon neutral cooking! Properly managed this little titbit would keep her secure in the hearts and minds of the electorate for as long as it suited her to be there.

London hadn't changed perceptibly when she returned to the capital two days later. The snow was piled in filthy heaps alongside the pavements. She'd pleaded that she needed to get her thoughts in order when Freddie suggested that she accompanied him to Chequers for a de-briefing. Ha-Ha!

His hackneyed joke sent her synapses into spasm. Maybe she would go down to Hampshire for the weekend. After that, the Minister of Power and Supply contemplated Monday morning's blood bath with joy in her heart.

WIND OF CHANGE

Joyce McKinney

I wake with a thumping headache to the rustle of the wind in the gum trees and the eerie creaking of the branches that tower as much as a hundred feet above our small house. Chania, our cocker spaniel, howls to be let in from the balcony outside our bedroom window.

I kick my legs to free myself from the rumpled damp sheets, thrust my feet into my sandals and thread my way through the boxes packed along the hall to open the front door. The dog darts past me towards the kitchen and I hear her empty metal bowl being pushed along the tiled floor to remind me it is time for breakfast. I rattle her food into the dish and go out onto the deck.

There is a haze and strange greyish-brown clouds hang low in the sky towards Kuringai north of us. A chopper passes overhead low enough to send up swirls of dry leaves and dust from our parched garden. I cover my face with my hands but I have smelled the smoke. It was there on the breeze when we went to bed and now there are scorched blackened leaves floating in the pool and littering the decking. It won't necessarily come to anything but I feel on edge. We have none of us slept well. It is much too hot.

The children moan and complain as I open their bedroom doors and shout at them to get up. I flick on the television weather channel to get the day's forecast – over forty, like yesterday, and strong winds increasing towards nightfall.

The French window, which I have not closed properly, crashes open and swirls of dust billow into the kitchen. As I run to fasten it I tread on the dog and she cowers under the table to stare out at me accusingly.

"What's up with Chania?" Brian asks. His eyes are red-rimmed from lack of sleep. I decide not to answer.

"One of us should stay home with you today."

"I'll do it," comes a voice from the corridor.

"You will not. She has an exam, Brian. Besides, I'll be fine. I'll drop the kids at the station and go to Miriam's for a coffee."

"You have ten minutes to get ready you two. Lunches are on the side table and I'm off to get the car. If you miss the train you can both walk."

"Yeah, yeah, yeah." I see Annabel's mouth moving but her words are lost in the heavy whir as another chopper passes on its way north. The noise is deafening and I rummage in the cupboard for a paracetamol.

"If you pack the good china in that box today leave it for me to lift when I get home." Brian makes for the door giving me a quick peck on the cheek as he passes.

"Hurry up you two. Don't keep your mother waiting."

The murky cloud of greyish smoke has almost extinguished the sun as I go down to fetch the car. My hands tremble as I struggle with the lock but I concentrate on what I am doing to avoid looking at the empty space beyond the garage. There is not much left of the Grahams' house and the plot is up for sale. Several families have come to look but there's a sad desolate air about the place and after two years there is still no word of a buyer. The garden is beginning to recover and I see small fresh shoots on the bushes and trees and soon the new growth will cover the blackened fallen timbers and it might then be easier to forget. I still miss them all but I could understand their wanting to move away.

I get home around midday. Brian phones to ask if I feel better and promises to get home early. He will bring more boxes for packing. Our warning code is still Amber so I have not to worry.

I plan a cold dinner – again. We none of us want hot food in this weather and I certainly don't want to heat up the kitchen by turning on the oven. I peep into Annabel's room but can't face the chaos of clothes for the washing basket, school books that have fallen off her desk and odd shoes and socks around her bed. I make myself do some packing of china but I am soon unbearably hot so I make for the lounge and sit there, cool drink in hand, the blinds drawn and the air-conditioning on. The dog comes and curls up beside me on the sofa.

There is a grey car down the creek road and the sound of people calling to each other when I come home with the children. I watch them drive up past our house, a youngish couple with small children in the back seat.

They are there again next day and Brian goes down to have a word with them when he comes home. Annabel tags along and soon comes back to say they are coming in for a drink.

The children clamour to be allowed to have a swim when they see the pool.

"They are bored and hot," – their mother is apologetic – "not much fun for them all this scrambling around in the bush."

The husband, Ben, is short and bouncy and immediately anxious to tell us about their plans to build down the hill. "We love the trees, don't we, Yvonne?" His wife smiles and nods in agreement. "And we can see how shady it is for you here. Beautiful."

We sit out by the pool as it begins to get dark. It is cooler there. Rain is promised so we look forward to the temperature dropping further during the night. Our children go off to find swimming gear for the visitors and come back with an assortment of costumes. They make a lot of noise splashing about together.

This is the best time of day before the mosquitoes begin to bite. The long slender tree barks shine white in the half-light and the birds swoop low near the water and land on the railings, sending the dog into a frenzy of barking. We have a couple of kookaburras that visit most evenings and they sit there cocking their heads at us, hunched like old men, as they wait for a bit of our dinner. Possums travel by on the lower tree branches as it gets darker and the movement activates the lights on the deck. They sit there illuminated with their babies on their backs, wide-eyed, staring at us for a while before they move on.

"We plan on building on the slope up this side of the creek," Ben tells us. "We'll put the house on the edge of the site and use the different levels to make an interesting layout. There are so many plans afoot to keep those wooded areas safe – but you'll know about all of that. We really feel they have things in hand now. The new fire chief has a lot of different ideas. Seems to be taking on board some of the Aborigine thinking on fire control. It all makes a lot of sense."

"Well, you have to listen to all that Abo shit these days." Brian is into his third beer and standing up, swinging his bottle about.

"I thought you were struck by what they had to say at that Council meeting," I ventured, and I saw Yvonne give a little smile. I liked her, wished they had come earlier. Brian could be insufferable at times. I knew he had agreed with so much that was being considered by the authorities. Everyone could see that those fires were getting bigger, more damaging and more difficult to control each year. In some areas people were anxious about their safety.

"I had no idea you were at the stage of having plans drawn up. You must have been looking at the site for a while."

"We have been back and forward for over a month now. Never ran into you though. We do love it here, don't we, Ben? We have walked all around and like it more each time we come."

No-one mentions the new house we have just rented. It doesn't seem to be the right time to tell them we mean to leave. I can't bring myself to spoil their enthusiasm for the place.

"What do you think of that then?" Brian asks me when they have gone. "It doesn't seem to worry them that this was an area at risk just a few years ago."

I shrug my shoulders.

Artwork by Jean Duncan RUA

Boat Track

A graduate of Edinburgh College of Art, Jean Duncan studied printmaking at Ulster Polytechnic Art and Design Centre. Her paintings and prints have been widely exhibited in Ireland, the UK and internationally. She is represented in many private and public collections including AIB Bank, Bank of Ireland, Arts Council of Northern Ireland, Dundee City Art Gallery, and the Department of Culture, Arts and the Gaeltacht. Elected to the Royal Ulster Academy in 1994, Duncan has been involved in the foundation of several of Northern Ireland's key cultural institutions. She is currently artist-in-residence with the Centre for Environmental Change and Human Resilience (CECHR) at the University of Dundee.

Field Sections

The Edge of the Field

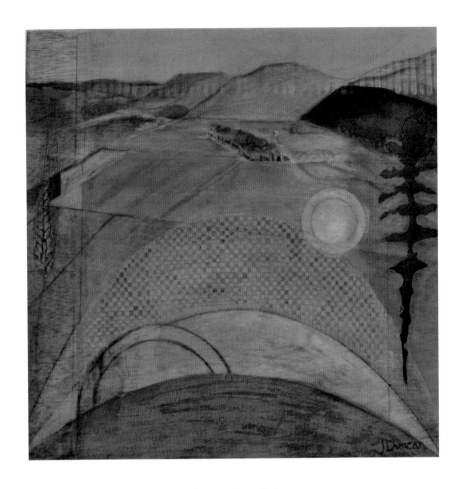

Kilmatin Glen

MAJOR INCIDENT AND THE MOOSHINERS

Roddie McKenzie

Dundee, 2070.

Jimmie Kirk pushed back his black beret, peered into the darkness of the Dighty Channel and strained to hear above the click of the cicidas. They were late, very late. The sweat trickled down his spine on this hot October evening. If the barrel train was not here soon, the moon would be up. He swung his binoculars round and leaned on the coaming of the conning tower of the *Milkshark* to scan the river. There were no vessels on the river – hostile or otherwise.

Just as well. They were stationary in just three metres of water. Since carbon taxes had been levied on all greenhouse gas-producing activities, smuggling was rife. One highly sought commodity was produced in the hidden glens of the Sidlaws and it funded, for Jimmie, the contraband that made life tolerable. That commodity came from one of the 'worst greenhouse gas criminals' – according to the World Action (for) Climate Optimisation, or WACO. Jimmie had often mused on this and the counter propaganda that he would tell his kids, but now he was interrupted by a whining voice like an out of tune fiddle.

"Mr Kirk?" Sandy the new apprentice clambered through the hatch and onto the running bridge.

Jimmie nodded.

Normally a farm hand and not the sharpest tool, it was Sandy's first voyage. Who would have thought that anyone as smart as Sandy's dad – deviser of the holographic camouflage that hid the farms – could produce someone as daft as Sandy?

"Why do the Feds hate coos?"

Jimmie ducked below the coaming to spark up a smoke. Nice aroma, he thought, Ochil Glens. Their warm summer slopes had been a great source of contraband dope but with the last four scorching summers they had added tobacco to their catalogue.

The rabbit eyes brought him back.

"It's no so much the coos, but whit comes oot their arses, Sandy."

"Well, eh kin understand that. Last herd we brought in filled the hold wi sae much dung that ma lass widnae speak tae me fur days efter eh shovelled it oot."

"Ach…Yer Da… he never sent ye tae the school that covered… Ach niverr mind – jist get the mooring lines ready."

"Aye, Mr Kirk." Sandy rubbed his nose and looked wide-eyed at Jimmie. "But who buys the mooshine?"

"Weel, the French like tae make a smelly food from the mooshine – Cammamboke – or something like that. When the European Federation make rules that they dinnae like, they just ignore them. So as long as yer Da's submarine can keep slipping past Major Incident's blockade, everyone's happy."

Then off Bridgefoot, Jimmie spotted a green lantern on the riverside. He jumped down the hatch into the engine deck where the sweet odour of the fish oil that lubricated the machinery swamped his nostrils after the mild musky perfume of the evening air.

"Scott, start her up, slow ahead."

"Aye Jimmie, but I think that's unfair. Ah ken ahm gittin on, but ah dinnae think ah'm slow in the heid."

Jimmie suppressed a laugh – the bugger was getting as deef as a door wi aw that engine-room noise.

"Scott… yer… ach never mind – jist listen for ma directions on the conning voice tube." He made a mental note to shout and turned to the ladder.

Scott looked disappointed and attempted to maintain the conversation. "How's the boss's boy's learning going, Jimmie?"

Jimmie bit his tongue and looked grave. "Aye he's getting therr, slowly," he said, adding, "but it's not knowledge as we know it, Scott."

As they drew in to the landing, Jimmie called for 'stop engines' and the twenty foot grey sub slowed gently into the earth berth. Sandy jumped ashore and made the lines fast to the bearded trunks of the ubiquitous Chusan palms. As Jimmie climbed down to the deck, a tall man slid with a rustle from the shadows of the twelve foot high bamboo grove.

"Hello, Captain, sorry we're late – had to lay up coming through the Seedlies for a bit till the gaugers passed and then a hobbled beast slowed us doon."

Jimmie looked him over, feeling the edginess beginning to flutter in his stomach. "What happened tae Eck?"

"Hulltoonbase Huns got him, last week."

Jimmie spat. "That's too bad, but dinnae worry, he'll no talk."

"He might if they ever manage to sober him up."

Jimmie laughed and felt the tension drop away.

"Aye, well ye ken Eck well enough."

"Captain, I'm Fergus, Fergus… Smith."

"Call me Jimmie – all the other Smiths do." They laughed, then shook hands.

"Okay, Jimmie, we have your cargo, thirty-six barrels, and two methane drums from the farm." He turned and indicated an ugly head protruding from the bamboo. The head was studded with two beady eyes that oscillated on a snaking neck.

"Bring them oot, Davie." A muscle-bound man in a camouflage T-shirt emerged from the foliage and pulled on a thin silver chain. An ostrich emerged, saddled by two twenty gallon barrels, netted and covered with foliage; the silver chain dipped back to another snaking shadow in the darkness. Soon twenty of the carnaptious beasts were lined up clawing and stamping on the riverbank accompanied by two other men who were tying the guide chain ends to the palm trunks.

"OK, Fergus, let's get her loaded." Jimmie spun the wheels that opened the forward hatch to the cargo hold and Smith's men began to unhitch the barrels from the pack train.

"Could a couple o yer lads gie us a hand wi unloading oor cargo?"

"Aye – Lennie, Keyso – gie the man a hand."

"Fergus, we're wan drum o Libyan crude less – it leaked and we hud tae… jettison it – wan ae yer beasts will hae an easy journey hame."

"Of course ye did," Fergus winked. "Nae disappointment fur the beast. We wur going tae eat the lame wan anyway."

"Yer a star, Fergus." Jimmie put on a scant grin. "Can you bring the methane drums over to aft deck, fellas."

Jimmie motioned to Sandy. "C'mon, we'll connect these to the refuelling rig on the stern. We might need the extra turbine pressure for a run to the sea. Get the tools, lad."

As they sat at the stern, Jimmie indicated the fuel drums.

"Right you need to learn to couple up the drums to the turbine intake."

"Whit?"

"The methane."

"Whit?"

"Yer supposed tae be training tae be an ingineer. Whit dae ye think maks this sub go?"

"Eh thought we jist opened the valves and the fart rushed oot and pushed us alang like that time Angus had an accident disconnecting the fart pants from the coos and he flew over the byre."

Jimmie growled and brushed a bead of sweat from his eyelid.

"Don't you ever look at that print-out that Ah gave ye? We compress farts intae the drums, then we burn the *methane* in them, in the turbine."

"Ah okay, so that's why we need to connect these hoses up to the drums. Ah thought that they farted away like jets on the stern."

"Naw, *these drums* are auxillary supplies fur emergencies. Opening this valve feeds the drum tae the turbines – no mind the talk ah gave ye about the mechanics o the sub?"

"Aye, sortie."

"Well, watch me dae this side." Jimmie strained on the spanner to loosen the coupling on the drum. "Then you can do the starboard side. But mak sure the couplings are on tight."

Meanwhile in Hulltoon Harbour, the shore protection base, the *Iron Lady* – a sixty foot smuggling and immigration interdiction vessel was preparing to cast off from the Multis Wharf. Major Commander Ahabi Incendio was on the bridge and in foul mood. Since their last capture, there had been a rain of slop bucket contents pouring down on the incoming crew from that crumbling, concrete tower overlooking the berth. In the light of the rising moon, it gleamed like a decayed tooth in the rotten mouth of this rottenest harbour in the EU Federation.

Then the choir started up with his ritual humiliation:

> *The wee I'Tally laddie*
> *Drove his boat sae badly.*
> *Flee'd aboot frae A tae B,*
> *Then clattered a rock aff Normandie.*

The Major's face flushed more vermillion than normal. His smoky hazel eyes peered in line with his raptor-beaked nose. His need for restitution was greater than ever and beat like a pulsing artery in his head.

"Why have the wind turbinators been de-activated?" he barked. Lieutenant Lamb turned and saluted.

"Sir, wind speed is too low to risk unnecessary wear on the bearing. As per standard operational divisional ecology measure (SODEM) 346, we will have to run on stored-battery power, sir!"

The Major pulled his clasped fingers down over his eyes in frustration.

"You – ah – mean tonight we can only make eight knots in this tub? Intelligencey says we probably will run into the milk runners."

"Yes, sir."

"Oh, for Godsake! Lieutenant Shee-ep! Shee-ep shagger? Whatever the fuck your name is… Get us out to the estu-aree to start the patrol."

The Major watched the lines flop into the harbour like fat seals and turned away to look out to the channel. He could pick out the red hazard lamps burning on the partially submerged road bridge. As the bow swung to starboard they lined up on a course parallel with the tidal reef lights marking the site of the swimming pool. Suddenly the lights went out across the town – Energy Saint Saver time. But the full moon had come up and the shadowy buildings of Dundee framed their course along the silvery Tay. He felt the deck rock gently in the swell as they picked up speed and headed east along the coast.

The forward hatch was secured and Jimmie had said goodbye to Fergus on casting off. They were underway, slow ahead.

"Have you finished connecting the barrels, Sandy?"

"Eh, but therr's…"

Jimmie started down the conning tower when Scott's voice drifted up from below.

"Jimmie, ye'd better listen tae this!"

Jimmie climbed back up and slid down the ladder. A few minutes later he emerged on the tower.

"Sandy, the Hulltooners have reported that a patrol vessel is leaving the quay heading east. We have to get down river into the Tay *now*. Stow the gear in the locker and get up here."

As if to emphasise his point the water foamed over the bow and swirled up like a predatory beast toward the deck. The water tsunamied over Sandy's shoes as he climbed the tower. They made full ahead with the spray whipping up around the tower base, past the winding channel at Claverhouse, the Isle of Fintry, tentatively past the shallows of the old Arbroath Road until at last they could see the right-hand curve of the channel as it joined the Tay beyond the Ferry Bank.

On the tower Jimmie breathed a sigh of relief. "Deep water, nearly there." He reached into his pocket and pulled out the Ochil Glens. He took one out, lit it and offered one to Sandy.

"Thanks, Mr Kirk." Sandy took a draw and pointed with the lit tip to a shadowy form standing off the bank behind them. "Is that the ship we are meeting?"

Jimmie followed the red pointer at the end of Sandy's arm. "Holy shit!" he muttered, then yelled down the voice tube. "Full ahead, Scott, head for the sea! They're waiting for us."

On the bridge of the *Iron Lady* the Major ordered full ahead, licking his lower lip exposing a wolfish grin. Glory beckoned. "We have them now! Get the turbinators on too – damn the SODEM!" Relentlessly the *Iron Lady* crept up on the *Milkshark*. "She can't escape – so no firing, cut her off, they know we have the– a– deptha charges," the Major announced over the intercom. Already he could see the victory celebrations as he towed the *Milkshark* into Rosyth Naval HQ. "Grappling magnets ready!" On the bow the deck crew loaded the huge air pistol with the magnet line rig.

On the running bridge of the *Milkshark* Jimmie and Sandy were chain-smoking as the distance closed. "Dammit, Scott, I need more speed."

"Captain, therr's nae mair speed left. Ye done aw the crystal last week. Onywey, dae ye think this is the right time fur that?"

"Naw! Ya doss deef half wit!"Jimmie roared. "Mak the boat go faster!"

"Captain! The engines are rid-hot, they canna take nae nair!"

"They're trying to intercept us. I'm going to cut in the reserve barrels. Prepare for the thrust." Turning away from the tube, he motioned to Sandy.

"Get doon on the aft deck and flip the valves on the reserve drums like ah showed ye. We need aw the speed we can get."

He watched as Sandy climbed down the ladder of the rolling tower, fag clamped between his lips. Sandy made his way first to the port side. As Sandy flipped the valve handles, the turbine roared and threw him backward against the barrels as their speed increased.

On the *Iron Duke* the Major noted the increasing speed of their quarry.

"They are going to pass us, they are getting away! Full ahead all turbinators to max power course to 160 degrees – ram them!"

"But Sir, the Ferry bank, it's dead ahead on that course."

"Lamb, you will never rise because you are scared of risk. They will hit us or we will hit them long before the bank. I won't let your scaredyness let victory slip away."

Sandy needed both hands to steady himself on the rocking deck as he leant over to flip the valve for the starboard barrels. He looked back in fear as the foaming bows of the *Iron Lady* raced in from their port side. As he flipped the valve, the sub lurched to port in an attempt to outrun the intercept. Sandy lurched starboard dropping his smoke. He was just aware of the hiss of gas through the loose couplings before the roar of ignition and the blue flame shot from the barrels. With all the thrust on the starboard side, the *Milkshark* turned at sixty degrees under the bows of the *Iron Lady,* the kick of the jet acceleration throwing Sandy against the port tanks as they roared into the channel just as the flame from the barrel expired.

On the bridge of the *Iron Lady* the Major Commander went from smile to bile in seconds as the *Milkshark* roared like a firework under their bows and out to sea. His mouth was still open as his ship ran at full speed up the Ferry bank.

Jimmie went aft to help a bleeding and bruised Sandy into the sub.

"MrKirk, Eh don't think Eh'm cut out to be a very guid ingeneer." Jimmie wrinkled his nose. He hated the pungent smell of burnt hair.

"Never mind laddie, ye've just had the best and biggest fart of yer life and it's an ill wind that blows naebody guid."

TILTING AT WINDMILLS

David Carson

Eleanor and her father sat in the kitchen, surrounded by boxes. The removal van was due to arrive in the afternoon. Neither spoke. Silence had become a habit. Eventually Eleanor said, "Why don't you take the wee one out in the buggy. He likes the fresh air."

"Aye."

The noise of the rotors echoed momentarily as he wheeled the buggy outside. He quickly closed the door behind him.

Eleanor looked out of the window. The view was the same – turbine shafts rising up to somewhere out of sight. Can it really be almost a year, she thought. I suppose I was lucky. For a while at any rate. She got up and poured some tea, then sat back down. She put her elbows on the table, cradling the cup in her hands. She stared into the distance, and the tea grew cold...

"Signed. Sealed. Done. Dusted." Eleanor's father, never prolix at the best of times, surpassed himself.

"And the delivery?"

He pulled an envelope from the inside of his jacket, and dropped it on the table. "In a month. Takes about six weeks. All in the contract."

"You don't think the field is a bit close to the house?"

"Windiest place. You know that. Trees had to come out. Before you were born."

So now we'll have a metal forest instead, thought Eleanor. And what would you have made of it all, Mum? she wondered. Pragmatic as ever, I bet. Your Dad is getting on, farming's not what it was, he can't rely on the weather any more, used to harvest crops, now he'll harvest electricity. You'll get used to it.

Easier said than done, thought Eleanor a few days later when massive lorries began to arrive. She watched in frozen fascination as they disgorged shafts, propellers, generators and rotors. Diggers ripped up the field and cranes manoeuvred the steel trunks into their foundations.

"It's like bloody Jack and the beanstalk out there," she said to her father one evening.

"Aye. But we're not stealing."

"I don't mean it that way. They're growing so quickly."

Her father shrugged. "Sooner the better."

"Did you know it was a French company doing the work?"

"No."

"At least, there's an engineer who's French. A real enthusiast. Name's Georges. Keeps trying to explain how the things work."

"Hot air, is it?"

Eleanor didn't expect a smile, and none came. "Like the speed of the propellers."

Her father said, "Don't distract him," which, Eleanor thought later, was unconsciously prescient.

"Eleanor, why do you keep staring out of the window. Come back to bed."

"I still can't get used to them, Georges. These past three years. I've tried. I look at them every day, hear them all the time. I've imagined them as sand-papered silver birches, giant organ pipes, and even robotic ballet dancers. But they're still just noisy ugly turbines."

Georges got up and stood behind Eleanor. He stroked her neck. She continued, "I keep thinking back to when the field was what it was for, a farm field with farm noises – snuffling sheep and stampeding cows."

"That world is not real any more. It's in the past." He put both arms round her, and stroked her stomach. "The future is what matters, for the three of us."

Eleanor looked down at her father, who was standing at the gate to the field, elbows on the topmost spar, his crook over his forearm. Sadie, ageing now, sat at his feet.

"I hope you're not forgetting him, Georges." She felt a lump rising in her throat. She knew there would be darkness in her father's eyes.

"Of course not. Even if he has not really approved of me."

"It's not that. It's just that he doesn't like change."

Georges smiled. "Sometimes you would think that he still had a farm to manage. The way he walks through the field with the dog, tapping the shafts with his stick, then telling us that everything is in order. It's bizarre."

Eleanor gave him a look. "You're one to talk. I've seen you out in the field, with that divining rod thing and your notebook. Maybe you'll explain one day.

Anyway, you shouldn't judge him like that. He's used to working hard all his life. He feels guilty, he thinks he should be out earning the money from the turbines. And he's becoming a real Calvinist."

"A what?"

"No pain no gain. The other day he said that the noise of the propellers is his penance for what they pay him. If that was the case, we should all be earning a fortune."

Georges looked puzzled. "I don't understand."

Eleanor pushed him gently in the chest. "Then you've grown turbine deaf. Are you immune to that racket, that penetrating repetitive throbbing? They say that babies in the womb are sensitive to noises round about. God help our wee one."

"No, we'll help our little one."

"Of course we will. But what do you mean exactly?"

"The changes that are happening, we have to try to understand them and use them for us." Georges moved from the window and started to pace up and down. "Especially the climate. There are opportunities, Eleanor. And yes, I have been doing some research. I am going to talk to you and your father about it tonight."

Eleanor smiled at Georges. "Ever the enthusiast."

That evening they sat round the kitchen table. The windows and shutters were closed, as much as against the raw October night as to muffle the beat of displaced air from the turbines.

"What's that?" Father pointed to a large sheet of paper that Georges had spread out on the table top.

"Research. Results. Rewards." You become like the people you live with, Eleanor thought.

Her father seemed bemused, and impatient. "Diagrams and figures. Meaning?"

Georges began to pace the length of the kitchen. He looked up at the ceiling, then turned his gaze on Eleanor and her father in turn.

"It's like a story, an adventure story, and it could only happen now," he stretched out his arms in an expansive, embracing gesture, "here, in that field, in that earth."

Eleanor's father drummed his fingers. "The point, if there is one."

"The point is truffles."

"And what are they?"

Georges looked shocked. "A cross between a mushroom and a potato, but more, much more than that. They are very valuable." He hurried on before further interruption. "Please continue to listen. It's very exciting." He turned to the sheet of paper on the table. "These figures in this column, they represent temperatures." He looked up. "Soil temperatures. Did you know that for over ten years your government has kept these statistics at different locations throughout the country?"

Eleanor shook her head. "They must have had a reason."

"Yes. To prove that this country is getting warmer."

Her father laughed. "Have you felt the temperature outside? Maybe things are different where you come from."

Eleanor glared at him, then turned to Georges. "Don't pay any attention. Father gets anxious about change. It can make him rude."

Georges shrugged. "Why do we not go to the field and I can show you what I mean?" Without waiting for a reply, he produced a torch from his pocket and opened the door. The moon had risen and the turbines seemed to hover high above in a bilious light. The drone of the propellers enveloped them. Eleanor shivered and folded her arms tightly across her front. The three figures moved cautiously over the field until Georges stopped underneath a turbine where the ground had been disturbed. He pointed at it. "This earth is several degrees warmer than it was ten years ago." He made a triumphant sweep of his arm.

"Doesn't feel like it tonight. Can't we go back inside?" Eleanor tugged at his arm.

"In a minute. I need to show you something else." He shone the torch round about the dislodged earth. "Do you see those roots?"

"Aye." Her father nodded. "From the old trees. The ones that used to be in the field. That were torn out."

"And do you remember what sort of trees they were?"

"Mixed. Beech. Poplar."

"But also pine and oak."

Georges squatted down and moved some earth away from them. "Just here is the ideal place to grow truffles. And last year I planted some acorns in these roots."

Eleanor's father stretched out his foot and began to push at the loose earth.

"No, not yet. Next week I will see if I have been successful."

Eleanor looked out from the window as Georges moved awkwardly across the field, spade in hand. Sadie followed him, nose to the ground. Over the last few days early snow had fallen, with frost at night. Hardly weather for truffle hunting, she had observed. But Georges had been adamant. "Snow protects the ground, keeps things warm."

Eleanor was not convinced, and as she watched him clear a path, she realised something was different. The field was quiet. The turbines had stopped. She peered up at the propellers, so high that they seemed to merge into the grey sky above. They were motionless. Unusual, she thought, to have them switched off. And then she realised that they were clogged – icy snow had built up between the blades.

She looked down, searching for Georges. He had reached the spot they had inspected the previous week. Georges began to thrust the spade into the ground. It seemed to bounce back. The ground must be hard. I told him so, Eleanor said aloud. Snow began to collect on the flat of the spade. Georges knocked it against the shaft of the turbine to dislodge it. Eleanor heard the dull clang of metal on metal. Sadie began to bark. Then Eleanor became aware of another noise, like a grating cough that turned into a pulsating clamour. And at the same moment that she realised the propellers had started to turn, she watched a solid block of oh-so-heavy iced-up snow fall at first in slow motion then at terrible speed. She managed to open the window just as it hit Georges, knocking him to the ground then burying him. Her frantic cries were lost in the implacable din that surrounded her.

Eleanor looked up with a start as the door opened and the buggy appeared, followed by her father. He slumped in his chair. He sighed.

"Maybe it was a punishment. For our greed."

"No father. Not that. It's like he said. Change. And chance."

"Even so. But I can't get rid of the thought. It turns round and round in my head."

Eleanor reached over and put her hand on his arm.

"We're doing the right thing."

Father and daughter looked at each other. Outside, the rhythmic beat broke like a tide against the walls of the house.

THE HOUSE

Fiona Duncan

So you wouldn't eat anyone, then?

The girl stared into nothing, her grey eyes mirroring the gelid water, the sky, the trees, black and burnt, like twigs from a witch's broom out of an old tale.

No.

She didn't look at the boy.

Not even if you were starving? You have to answer me.

The slow turning of a head as she scanned the dark and ravaged land. Nothing moved. Only an ashy wind rattled brittle, blackened leaves on long dead branches.

No. And we are starving.

The boy, matted hair falling in greasy strands over a waxen face, put his hands into his armpits to warm himself. He was shivering so badly she could see his eyelashes tremble on blue-veined skin. He had taken off his pack and left it on the ground. She knew exactly what it contained. Not much. He was so thin now he had no energy to carry more. And every day they had less. She went through the inventory in her head as he drew in the dark dust that settled everywhere with a pitted metal spike he'd picked up. Sleeping bag, blanket, candles, lighter, three bars of soap she'd scavenged from the Apex Hotel before it became too dangerous to go in, a plastic figure of Spiderman, a pack of cards, six miniature packs of cereal, also from the Apex, three ring pull cans of pasta shapes. She carried more, because she was older and stronger. Medical supplies, some tools and string, a stove and a small bottle of precious oil and a plastic tarp to cover them when it rained. More food. Some water. But they had to get more food.

No. We're not starving. We've got food.

Not much, though. We need to find more.

In the old days food used to grow, didn't it?

He sounded curious, not regretful, as if he was talking of a fabulous land of myth and legend, a land that would never again exist. A land he did not even remember. She pulled him into her, holding him tight for a minute and kissed his head. He smelt like a wet dog. But there were no dogs now either. No food that grew, no dogs.

Yes, it did. But not now. And not again.

So we have to go in here? We have to search and look hard?

Yes, but we have to be careful.

She raised her head and looked again at the house. It was an isolated place, further out than they'd been before, at the end of the Perth Road, but hunger had forced her hand. They were down to the last now. Maybe three more days. Or four. Then unless she found something…

Lie down under that tree. No, in the ditch there. It's dry. Put your mask on. Wait till I come out. Don't move. Hide if you hear anyone.

She took off her pack and stored it in the ditch beside him. He looked at her, his eyes huge, those sharp cheek bones, a red spot on each white cheek, his filthy, ragged coat dragging the cold earth.

I can come. I can help. I'm old enough.

Her heart should have died along with the world. There was no place for this pity and sorrow in the cold new order of things.

Someone has to look out for our stuff. We lose that we die. It's important.

She laid her hand on his head.

I'm taking the knife. But I won't need it. I'm coming back. I won't leave you. We look after each other. That's what we do.

She held his stick arms, heart-breakingly fragile, like the bones of a broken bird, and looked at him straight so that he'd believe her.

I wouldn't lie.

OK, then. OK.

He climbed down into the harsh blackened stalks and grainy earth, the smell of death and mould around him.

Stay down. Stay hidden.

She wanted to tell him. If I don't come back, this is what you do. But she knew he would panic and not remember. Well, if she didn't return, that would be it. She wouldn't know.

Crawling forwards towards the house she felt uneasily exposed. She tried not to think about the gangs of bone eaters and their sickening fires, who had colonised the hotels in the city. Surely they wouldn't come out so far. The place looked dead. No smoke. No ashy tracks to the front door. The windows were intact but grimed with the sooty dusty spores that smeared everything, streaked and bleary where black rain had fallen from lowering, disinterested skies. The door, scabbed and peeling, was partly open, leaves wedged in the gap. They looked undisturbed, as if they'd blown there and settled and no one had walked on them. A rare faint hope rose in her then. A feeling so alien she hardly recognised it.

She inched forward in the harsh grass until she reached the door where she crouched up and, heart pounding, pushed. A second door inside, stained glass patterns hidden under layers of dirt. Stepping carefully over buckled boards she headed for the kitchen. A table set with knives, forks and plates. Napkins curled in streaked glasses, reminding her of the life before. A tea towel on a hook. Oven gloves. Dead plants on a windowsill. The house looked untouched. She ignored the fridge, for with no power everything in there would be useless, clogged with mould and fungus, and made straight for the cupboards.

In the first, hopeless, beautiful dishes blue painted with birds. No birds now. He hadn't even seen a bird, except in a book. They seemed like mythical creatures to him, yet once they'd been everywhere. But it was quiet in the world now. The next cupboard, tins. And packets. Her throat closed and she choked back tears. Taking each precious can down, she checked the labels: pears, peaches, pineapples. Too many to count. In the next cupboard, more cans: chilli, curry, beef, tuna. And more. Carefully she stacked the food on the counters beside corroding appliances, useless without the power that had now been switched off forever. A radio. She touched the dial for a moment, hearing long dead voices in her head, then went to tell her brother the good news.

They wouldn't starve. Not yet. Maybe they could stay in the house for a while. Unless the family lay dead and crumbling in the rooms upstairs. Even then. She could take the blankets; make a nest for them in the downstairs rooms. Make sure no smoke showed. Barricade the doors. It would be fine. For a while. Until the food ran out. Or someone came as she had done and took it from them. It was the best she could hope for. In the dying world they'd inherited, it was the best she could do.

LA VITA È BELLA
LIFE IS BEAUTIFUL

June Cadden

My children, of course, recycled everything in sight. Sometimes I could see them eying up the packaging of my meal deal sandwich. It was quite a pressure knowing that at the last bite the cardboard would be wrenched from my hands. But it wasn't until Tarquin started going on about how I didn't care about my grandchildren's future that I really got the 'save-the-planet' bug.

It was when I was contemplating what contribution I could make that I thought about my toe-nail cuttings. I knew that I should be recycling them but where – in with the grass or in with the plastics? I googled it and there were plenty of helpful suggestions such as putting them into the bottom of plant pots, using them in an embroidery montage or even putting a good collection of them into an old pair of tights, knotting them and then using the item as an eco-friendly pot scourer. I'd have to start collecting them now, though, if that was my preferred option as my own collection would never be enough.

In the meantime I decided to ring the council since the number was on the leaflet that came with the recycling boxes. It said 'get helpful advice; no question too trivial, recycle before it's too late'. The last bit did worry me a bit. Did 'too late' mean that the office closed early or did it mean that Armageddon had been pencilled in for next week? Anyway the conversation went a bit like this:

"Is that the recycling advice line?" I asked.

"Yes," came the less than friendly reply.

"I was just wondering which box I should put my toe-nails into." There was a pause before he said:

"And do you intend to get in with them, madam?"

Well, I won't report the rest but it didn't give me confidence. This was turning out to be a very negative day. Firstly I'd received a curt text from my son inferring that I had lost it and now the man from the council had almost said the same thing at the end of our question and answer session. It was definitely time to get the crystal out of my pocket and give it a quick caress.

However, I knew that things had become serious when Sid, my husband, also got the save-the-planet bug. He's a man of few words is Sid but even he began to be affected by reports in the media and would read out the headlines from the paper whilst I was busy getting the tea ready: *Water to run out in fifty years time. Wars will be fought over scarce water supplies.* Made me depressed really but it all made sense and I knew what to do – no more baths for us and no more using the bidet. It did look a bit redundant next to the loo but I soon found the solution – plant the aspidistra in it. A stroke of genius it was as the aspidistra has never looked so healthy. It took a bit of getting used to but you can get used to anything really if you put your mind to it. That's what my friend Sal says, and she should know; she's a real eccentric is Sal.

And I still had Sid's birthday to look forward to. I rang my son to discuss the options. I shouldn't have tried to involve him. I know that now but I just wished that he hadn't spoken to me as he did. So condescending. Not exactly encouraging.

"It's all very well for you to say that," I told him, "but it's a bit late now. It's all paid for and it's on its way."

I heard the sigh, well more than heard it; I felt as if I was being sucked down the line with the strength of his intake of breath.

"Keep me informed," he said to me in a bored on-your-own-head-be-it tone of voice.

Despite Tarquin's reservations – and his refusal to be present to see Sid's reaction – I had to admit that I was getting really excited. This birthday was going to be something special. Even without Tarquin's help everything was fitting into place quite nicely. Thankfully our garage is not attached to the house as that could have made things difficult and Sid's often away on business. Sal, bless, came and gave me a hand when I needed it to transform the garage and she patted my hand when it all became a bit much. I don't know what I would have done without her.

And then the big day came! I had to blindfold Sid or it wouldn't have been such a surprise. I took his hand and we made our way out of the house to the side door of the garage. I carefully opened the door, led him in, put on the light and took his blindfold off.

"Jesus bloody Christ," is what I think he said as he surveyed the scene. "Bloody hell, Syb, have you totally lost it or is this some sick joke for Christmas? Where's my car? And where do the chickens fit into the Nativity?"

"Oh, I sold the car," I told Sid. "I mean, where would I have put the calf if we still had the car? You said yourself that we needed to cut our carbon footprint. This way we can still fly and no longer feel guilty about it. Anyway, think positive, now we'll have fresh milk. Well, we will have once I've got the hang of how to milk our Daisy. No more worries about the use-by dates. And once the hens start to lay – fresh eggs as well. Of course, I'd like you to make a run for them. They can't stay here or they might stress out Daisy."

I looked at Sid. He opened his mouth to say something but the words never came. He closed his mouth and made his way back into the house, a bit dazed.

"So, do you like your birthday present then?" I asked him. "I named the calf but I've left the chickens for you to name. It's thanks to you that we have this lot. I wouldn't have got the idea had you not kept telling me that we should be careful about what we eat."

In time, I got the hang of the milking. It took a lot longer, however, to convince the hens to lay round eggs instead of the misshapen offerings they gave us at first. But then, what's life, if not a challenge?

I have to say that I am disappointed in the children. I thought they would be proud of us, but I have a sneaky feeling that we're a bit of an embarrassment to them.

However, they say that good things never last – and it's true. Sal turned up today and said that she had some worrying news. She'd heard it on the radio that morning. It turns out that we had swopped the carbon emissions of the car for the methane gasses of our cow and Daisy produced more than the Peugeot. Well, that's what Sal said. There was only one solution.

Sid and I shed a few tears but we know that we made the right decision. It did turn out to be a bit of a struggle as it took us about four months to get through Daisy. I've never eaten so much boeuf bourguignon in my life. Still, I comforted myself in the knowledge that all the ingredients were organic. It was, however, a bit of a shock when the next electricity bill arrived. It turned out that the power that we had used to cook, freeze and preserve Daisy for our consumption had made more demands on the eco-system than Daisy ever did. Oh well, it was going to have to be home-made presents for Christmas. I had already been thinking of recycled paper bricks for open fires. I would have to dye them, of course, with leaves from the compost heap to give them that festive touch and I just had to hope that the less than attractive smell would evaporate before the 25th December.

Anyway, that was five years ago now and Sid and I have grown very accustomed to our fresh eggs and milk. Of course when the odd chicken dies we do recycle it – on the barbecue as it happens. The children aren't that keen on that side of things. I have tried to explain the life cycle to them but they're not really interested.

Of course, we're vegetarian now and the garden's gone. We've got our own market garden. I don't regret a thing. Well, that's not completely true; I do sometimes have doubts as to whether Sid and my combined gasses are more than those that Daisy produced. I can't let myself think too long and hard about this or I would have to come to the inevitable conclusion. Sid would have to go. Still, best not to make a hasty decision. Oh, and we now make our own wine – parsnip as it turns out. It has a real kick. So, you see I've come a long way since the phone call to the council. Oh happy days.

THE RIVER

Chris Smith

It would all change with the visit of Mark Twain, a man who could see the brown waters and wax lyrical. He'd arrive in his charabanc with his party en route to a speaking engagement at St Andrews. Stepping out in the farmyard, he'd wave his entourage away as we walked down the field toward the Tay.

Leaning on the gate at the edge where the bank tilted down to the river, he'd pull out his pipe. Tapping it out, he'd refill it and light up. Then the words would come, tumbling out like quicksilver over pebbles, words which flutter behind and find me chasing to catch and hold one or two.

"Mighty fine river, you've got there… Man could find himself and just about anybody else he wanted to be in his day to day travails. Y'know, it was Horace Bixby showed me a river that brought me to this." He'd gesture, palms open and wide.

I look out from our bedroom in bright sunshine. At the horizon where the river meets the sky, there is the accent of a silver thread. During the day, these are the bridges.

My neighbour, brought up in this house, tells a story. As a youngster, in the gloaming, his uncle would swear the twinkling lights of far off Dundee were where the fairies stayed. Nowadays, our fairies work on oil derricks in Camperdown docks spraying orange into the night.

In the middle distance, the blue elbow of the river touches where the Picts of Newburgh came to live. Early settlements tell us they came to fish and farm. All their days were spent in staying alive.

In the shorter distance, there is a wood where the Romans built a fort and held court. Their records tell us they came to tax and rule. All their days were spent in staying alive.

Every day over the year, I walk out over the fields. In the frozen clods of February, I jump from furrow to furrow moving along the contours. As the early afternoon sunshine slants across the concentric lines, it is easy to see where the old river level used to lap twice a day. If you are going to drop anything, it's always when you are getting in or out of a boat but the men with metal detectors forage around today's tides in vain. They generally stomp off empty-handed and muddy. The farmer ploughing deep has often been the inadvertent treasurer hunter. The Roman coin is then displayed on the mantelpiece until it gets taken to the primary school and its first public exposure in centuries.

From the high shoulder of the field, I look out across the reed beds which form a margin. Once used for thatch, the reeds were farmed by cheery men with large scythes on improbable wheeled machines. Now, the whole is conserved as a site of scientific interest. Waterfowl disappear into its midst and deer crash across its heart. The dark uncertainty of black greasy water at the stalks' base means I would have to be braver than I am to venture too far into this maize.

Later in the year, the marsh harriers and red kites will be braver. Hunting alongside the buzzards and ospreys, they will ignore our instructions about electricity pylons. Perching on and swooping around these structures, the raptors clearly did not get the memo.

Every morning in the summer months, the osprey will flap up the Tay and break off at the confluence of the Earn. It heads upland towards Abernethy and disappears off towards the wind turbines beyond Glenfarg. For us, it is unremarkable in its regularity until a visitor in the house bursts into the kitchen.

"Have you seen that golden eagle... it's a huge eagle... bird thing," says the man whose connection with the outdoor world is a BBC Naturewatch TV programme.

Cue casual glance at watch. "10.30. That'll be the osprey."

However, it's really only those who would manage nature who are in love with schedules and clipboards. They fret on our behalf. They are spring-loaded to object for everyone's sake. And the river doesn't listen.

Victorian farmers threw men and effort into field drains to create better land for crops. As I squelch across a boot-grabbing trench, the river, the rain and rising water table smirk.

After heavy rain, a spate and high tide, the river impersonates the Ganges for me. Like images from a childhood National Geographic, I see large trees as petrified dinosaur cadavers flowing slowly in the ebb. Crows, astride, peck away. All reforestation is temporary, whispers the river.

I recall the tale of an Orcadian who moved to the Western Isles, taking over an abandoned black house. As he set about renovating the place, his absence at the church on Sunday was noticed by the elders. One of them dutifully called on the new islander on a Sunday morning to gently remind him of the Lord's invitation to attend that morning's service. He found the Orcadian hard at work in the overgrown garden and said, "You are working on the Lord's Day."

"Aye. The previous tenant left this garden to His care and see the mess He made of it. I am just helping Him put it right."

The wind turbines in the eastern sky line tickle me. They remind me of a crocodile line of primary school children waving their hands. I forget to remember that they don't work all the time 'because the wind doesn't blow all the time'. Tell that to my poor apple trees all asymmetrically lopsided on the windward side from the prevailing westerlies. I ignore the piles of dead birds piled around their bases which must surely form some grisly guano corpse pyramid in time. One night I will sit and await the mysterious night workers who come and scrupulously tidy in the dark hours. Equally, I am deaf to the subsonic noise vibrations which will surely cause my ears to bleed. Like a happy simpleton, I look at the happy windmills and smile for their cheery company. Doubtless, the rhythmic tips are working some voodoo magic to bring me into their sway.

But the river lets me turn away from Babel. Its people speak one language in many forms. The lady with the laughing eyes who pulls her life's tales out like a magician pulling coloured scarf after coloured scarf from his top hat, she worked in the inn, which was next to the pier that was used by the ferry and the fishing. So she talks of times when Sundays were full of pints for 'bona fide travellers', of Newburgh men who would, of necessity, walk to Abernethy for their 'bona fides' and vice versa.

And then, the ferries. One would go from the inn, to Newburgh and to Dundee. The other, more casual, simply plied across the Tay. Up from the fishing bothy, a traveller with a white handkerchief would wave across their pick-up request. The ferry would be dispatched, a woman on the oars. The men would be away at the fishing. Legend had it Macduff crossed and, having no Caley dosh, chose to pay with a loaf. The inn for a while was then known as 'the Inn of the Loaf'.

And then, the fishing. But, important to note, the net fishing. Not rod, cast, angler or fly. We're at the nets. Every one did it differently nevertheless. The Tay Salmon boys did it one way, the private 'uns did it their way. Stories and characters, as you would imagine, fill every crevice in the tales, the hands, once more alive, as nets are cast and followed.

"The thing is to let the net rest. There's a wee hollow, where the fish, in the tide, would lie. Let the net rest with them. And gently to follow the coble. Me from the shore. Just knowing the right pace."

The same pace on the shore from February until October twice a day with tides moving one hour each day. No computers or plotted tidal tables; the simple rhythm of a working life which was based on effort, the effort of the moon on tide and gravity on river and man's effort to work alongside. Many men had to sleep alongside the river to be ready to make the effort. Over 200 odd bothies were spaced along the river to provide the shortest commute to work.

The longest commute to life was the salmon's. From the far oceans to spawn in the far north river, this chain had many links. Some broke. Whether it was at sea or the moving sandbanks in the river; the effect was man's effort started to bear decreasing reward. He stepped away from the river as the famers stepped away from the land. The river became a quiet place that welcomed islanders like myself.

I was brought up with rivers, called by First Nations and French colonials, Manotick and Rideau. Canoed in summer and skated in winter.

Faced with my own river in my back yard, the Canadian canoe arrived. In our first jaunt, I stepped into the open deck, rolled the boat and capsized my wife. Spitting brown water and weed, she made for the house. She informed me she had misplaced her mobile phone or something similar. I didn't realise Nokia had an Effing range, but after six hours and a low tide, it reappeared in ceramic blue on a bed of ochre silt. If she was still talking to me at the time, I would have told her, by Nokia Effing phone, that all was well and reception was pretty good from the mudflats.

The next time, I have an oar in my hand; there are three other young men with oars and a man with a tiller in his hand. In a coastal skiff, built by the skelfs in our fingers and the sweat of our builders' cleavage, we will do battle with like-minded others on the river. In good weather, on a favourable tide, with little or no wind.

"You'll no have to beast it boys, ken. Ken, pull together. Watch they lasses. They sorta slide it along together, ken." The cox, our man with the plan, is a good man from river pilot stock. He helped plan the building of the boat in the yard where net boats and coble used to be repaired during the winter.

Today, at the regatta, he watches as young women jump into skiffs and reap the benefits of physics and a collaborative nature. Their better power to weight ratio equates to less drag and they selflessly pull in unison with little or no encouragement. They whizz along the surface with insect boatmen as the young men grunt, curse and chop into waves that plume above the gunwale.

As we finish the long hard pull and drift into the shallow jetty, the lads complain and dig each other up as they light their cigarettes. The other jetty still has the flowers tied to the railings. The river and young men are uneasy together.

The secrets of the river don't sit easy either. The badger sets, the deer, the ospreys, the beaver, the otters and seals all have our omerta. The 5000 year old long boat found in the mud at Carpow was known to generations of local youngsters who had secret dens and forts before it was first discovered by someone with a clipboard in 2001. They took it away and put it on show so people could not be seduced by the river. In a dimly lit room, with big words on a panel to interpret and engage you, and with a man in a uniform standing there to prevent you touching it: this is your history.

I am standing on a bluff, smelling rain, in a breeze, and wondering. It's all changing and, yet to me , it remains the same.

In the distance, I see two figures approaching. One of them has a clipboard.

ROOTS

Janice Thomson

The bothy door was unlocked. As expected. Dr Robert MacLean glanced at the rusted oval disk on the cottage door. The historic inscription announced 'MBA' and around the base in explanation, 'Mountain Bothies Association'. A'Chuil was typical of its type – old estate houses rescued from ruin by volunteers back in the 1960s and used as shelters for the hillgoing fraternity of that era, now preserved as national museums. Not that many folk ventured out this far in the remote country. The glen was of course on a TC and he knew the Through Corridors were relatively safe. Of course he had had to apply for a permit; the usual red tape stuff. And his vaccination against Lyme disease was always up to date ready for these forays.

Robert lifted the latch of the heavy wooden door and stepped into the past. In the small hallway were the bothy tools. A coarse sweeping brush, a curved wood saw hanging from a bent nail and propped in the corner against the rough stonework of the outer wall, the spade for 'toilet duties'. Two doors led off. One opened into a room with a raised sleeping platform which ran the length of one side. Opposite, a grimy curtainless sash window and on the gable end a smoke-blackened fireplace. He retraced his steps to the other room; much the same size and style.

The survival canisters, ordered before he left the office, stood by the door. The maintenance team would be well on their way back to base. Few of them had his passion and love for the wilderness. He would get the place to himself. He would savour the aloneness. At least until tomorrow.

He peered through the web-clad window at the gathering gloom. The steep flank of Sgurr Coireachan loomed over the forest which dressed the floor of the glen. He lifted the saw from its hook and stepped out into the highland dusk. He needed to experience what they had known.

A movement ahead. He hesitated, breath held. Slowly he reached for the stun gun on his hip. He had seen wolves in the distance but they were not a great concern. They hunted in packs and could bring down a full-sized red deer. There was plenty of easy prey and humans were given a wide berth. Same for lynx, though he had never so much as caught a glimpse of the big cat. Wild boar were a different matter and he had heard of attacks when they had been disturbed in their woodland environment. His eyes adjusted as he scanned the darkening scene. Three young hinds were grazing over by the trees. They caught his scent, turned, alert, motionless then darted deep among the pines. His heartbeat quietened, eased.

Robert smiled. His fellow professors in the Scottish Studies Department at Balmoral thought him quite mad. And he was content to be viewed so. As Chair, he was given as much time for research and field work as he pestered for. And he was more than pleased for others to teach the unenthusiastic young multitude from the industrial belt.

Nowadays his expertise in mountain flora and fauna was acknowledged worldwide. He had been head-hunted as Senior Consultant for the government-sponsored Highland Regeneration Programme. His eyes were drawn upwards as he thought of the decommissioning work and tomorrow's assignation.

Robert gathered an armful of fallen branches. He would set a good fire and ensure a warm night's sleep. It was dark when he arrived back.

The fire crackled. Above, on the mantelshelf, four stumps of candles flickered sharp shadows on the wood-panelled walls. He sat gazing into the fire's heart, transfixed, the flames hypnotic. Then that sense of something – a presence – enveloped him. Benign, non-threatening. It had never frightened him. He reached into the rucksack by his side and withdrew the battered old book and read.

Dawn woke him through the skylight. He dressed and strode across to the front window. The sun was not yet over the mountain but it promised to be a fine day. Only the faint whisper of a breeze rippling the reeds by the burn disturbed the stillness. Gear checked and stowed, he hefted the rucksack onto his back, fastened the hip belt and stepped outside. He sucked in the sharp coolness of the morning. Above the forest Sgurr Coireachan was veiled in shade. As was the outcome of this meeting, he mused. Yes, he viewed the national decommissioning programme as progress. Time and power technology had moved on. Repopulation of the Highlands was now a government priority. He had not been surprised to be asked to play a major role in the land restoration. He had expected it. No one knew this place better than he. Its vulnerability. The interwoven elements of a fragile landscape. His task was to oversee his land's re-flowering... he liked the sound of that. He would use it at the meeting. But to support a project for a tourism centre atop one of the country's most iconic mountains...

"... *scheduled for 12 noon... John Galbraith from Wellington NZ will be flown to the site by helicopter... Please assist, advise, report... welcome him."*

Robert had picked up the message in his office a few days earlier. He knew the name of course. And the company *Galbraith Global.* Galbraith: mega rich globe trotter, famed and infamous for setting up leisure and tourism businesses worldwide. A trawl through the online archives had thrown up something altogether more interesting, and possibly useful, he thought. Later, in the library, he had tracked down the bothy book.

A burst of Golden Saxifrage clinging to the bank of a pool beckoned him to sit. He sank his fist into the crystal depth, scooping the iced water onto his face, the cold sting of it soothing his mood. He glanced around the familiar terrain, identifying, taking pleasure in mouthing the names of plants and feeling the poetry. "Calluna vulgaris, Erica cinerea, Erica tetralix, Vaccinium myrtillus..." He rhymed off dozens close to where he sat, till the midge cloud got scent of him and forced him to continue his ascent.

He reached the summit plateau at 11.30am, his boots crunching ashen footprints in the charred turf. Heading for the Admin Cabin he passed a team of welders – the metallic clank and roar of the cutters, sputtered embers emitting the acrid smell of smoke and flame. Felled turbines lay twisted, grotesque. Over the cacophony, Robert could just pick up the *wap wap, wap wap* of the chopper as it took off from the helipad. So he was already here.

"He's out back!" was the shouted reply to his enquiry.

Robert stood watching the man. His back was turned and he was examining one of Robert's vegetation carpets rolled up on the ground behind the cabin.

His shouted, "Hello, Mr Galbraith!" carried above the din and brought a swift response. The figure rose, swiftly turned and strode towards him proffering his hand.

"Hi there. It's John. You must be Robert. Great to meet you. Really appreciate your time."

The handshake was as brisk and clipped as the voice. But there was unexpected warmth and sincerity in the strong grip, Robert felt, in spite of the practised charm.

"My people tell me this site is ripe for development. GG can do great things here; bring back your tourists, economy viable again... great place, great place. My roots are here you know."

Robert watched Galbraith as his eyes darted around the area.

"We'll bring a funicular and chairlifts up this side." He gestured wildly in the direction of the northern aspect of the mountain. They looked down at the zigzag gashes of vehicular access tracks, deep grey gouges on a contouring crawl upwards. "Proper roadways… parking." His gaze returned to sweep the plateau.

Robert followed in Galbraith's wake as he marched amongst the mangled metal.

"Mountain theme park, visitor centre, museum, shops, restaurant… all state of the art, state of the art." A sudden cessation of movement and he turned unsmiling. "The powers at Holyrood need assurance that the land will be put back as it was – around the theme park that is. Vegetation back to normal. Whatever that means. Your specialism. I need your rubber stamp on that for the go-ahead. Naturally, as my local adviser you'll be more than adequately remunerated when the work gets underway. And of course it's a roll-out project, and I want you along. Feasibility tests are being carried out in Glen Shee and at Torridon. So you can see the potential, Robert."

Robert rode the uneasy lull that followed. He scanned the horizon, now virtually free of ironmongery, his whole being absorbing the distant, lonely peaks, darkly purple in the gloaming; U-shaped valleys cupping steely ribbon lochs, high corries spewing violent strips of white gems. He sensed Galbraith watching, waiting. He turned to face the man. "Yes, I see what you mean."

"Good, good. I hate to lose when I can see the benefits of a plan – to all concerned. At the same time I won't fight for it. I don't need to. There's plenty of worldwide fish to fry." Galbraith moved towards the Admin Cabin.

John Galbraith had been quick to agree to Robert's suggestion. Descend to A'Chuil. A good opportunity to get the lie of the land, explained Robert. Get the feel of the place. The bothy would be quiet, a private venue for further discussion. Galbraith had immediately contacted his pilot to pick him up at a clearing further down the valley the following day. "… collect at 0600 hours, grid ref 979 914."

On the way down, at Galbraith's request, Robert had talked to him about his work. He had described geographical features, pointed out the effects of glaciation, named grasses, lichens, ferns, mosses, flowers. Robert had been surprised at the man's interest. They had walked for spells in companionable silence then shared a flask of coffee by a lochan. They sat by the peat dark water longer than Robert had anticipated. Galbraith had nodded off, head supported by a clump of auburn deer grass.

Robert sensed the encroaching dusk, felt the chill rise from the pool that moments before had sparkled warmth. "Time to go, John." From the outflow, at the southern lip, Robert followed the gurgling burn's course towards the glen. This was his world, his element and Galbraith was being gently reeled in. He would tell him about their grandfathers later – over a few drams, of course.

As they approached A'Chuil Galbraith stopped abruptly. His arm swept, gathering the landscape towards himself. "To think that this is the country of my forefathers. I can't help feeling a sense of belonging. Isn't that strange?"

Robert knew it was time. "Right here," he stabbed his forefinger at the ground, "you are walking in your grandfather John's footsteps." Galbraith's eyes widened as he absorbed the information which Robert poured forth. Of the years their grandfathers had spent together walking these very hills. How back in the days of 'Right to Roam' and Access legislation their interest and involvement in the mountains and conservation issues had developed along with the depth of their friendship. A friendship severed when John Galbraith emigrated following the demise of his hotel business. "Like a repeat of the early Highland Clearances. The wind farms crippled the tourist industry," Robert explained. "Oh, there was plenty of campaigning, but it all went ahead anyway."

A cool evening breeze stirred the reeds in the valley floor. They moved through squelching bog land to the shelter of the cottage. Robert left Galbraith to explore the interior of the house. He selected a couple of the dehydrated meals from one of the survival canisters and set to the preparation. Fresh water from another of the canisters was soon heated in the Jetboil stove.

After dinner, Robert's hipflask passed between them; the Drumgoyne sharp, warm, welcome. The bothy book, opened at the appropriate page, he handed to Galbraith.

16th May 1984

Arrived A'Chuil 5pm after long weary walk-in. We almost walked past it again. Really have to keep a sharp look-out for the path that leads off the main track down through the forest to where it's hidden. But we're never disappointed when we arrive. The cottage looks out over a clearing towards the woods – so there's plenty of stuff for the fire lying about. There's a wee burn to the east side of the house close by for drinking water.

Bothy clean and all mod con as usual. Had a fire going in no time. Early bed for us tonight, after dinner and a few drams of course. Tomorrow is a big hill day… four Munros!

John Galbraith and Bob MacLean – Highlanders Climbing Club

The two men sat, legs stretched, feet perched on the grate. Neither spoke. The clicking embers signalled the dying fire. Robert broke the spell. "What would

ROOTS

they have wanted for the mountains, do you think? *Our* mountains, *our* inheritance."
He paused. The window rattled its resistance to the heightening north-westerlies.
"There's a way of channelling your resources, John, enhancing the tourism
opportunities while minimising the impact on the mountains."

Galbraith turned, questioning, his face glowing. The heat of the fire, the
Malt... or something else, Robert wondered.

Into the wee, small hours they talked, argued, shared information –
*"national parks, pristine mountains, valley tourism sites, guided access, wildlife treks, boar
hunting..."* Neither slept much. Galbraith told him he had felt a presence.

They left the bothy at daybreak. Dawn had thrown a giant tablecloth over
Sgurr Coireachan. The sun had yet to show face but it promised to be a fine day.
Only the *wap wap, wap wap* of the rotor blades disturbed the stillness.

SEAWEED AND COTTON

Fiona Pretswell

Marcus was nervous. He could smell the perspiration rising from his pores as he walked towards the Magistrum's door. The order to appear here had come just before the end of his shift. He knocked. A voice boomed from inside. "Come." Marcus pushed the metal door, its touch cold beneath his hand; the smell of the steel stinging the back of his throat.

"Ah Marcus, my young warrior. Come. Sit."

A giant of a man rose from his leather-bound chair and extended his hand to Marcus. Marcus gulped. He had only met the head of the Authority in Dundee once before when he was a child. The man had scared him then and he did again. Except now Marcus hoped that he was pleased with him.

"I wanted to speak to you in person. To explain to you the path the Authority has chosen for you." Marcus stood tall, his eyes focused directly on the Magistrum.

"Your test results are back. Your genes are pure. There are no recessive tendencies. Your genes have the full superior specific alleles. You, my young man, are exquisite." Marcus felt himself turn red and he could feel the adrenalin in his veins. Suddenly the telephone rang and the Magistrum quickly reached to answer it. After a few words he turned sharply to Marcus, waving him out of the room with an instruction to return at the same time tomorrow.

The sunlight was beginning to creep up the river, catching the fine ash particles in the air and turning the morning sky a pale ruby red as Marcus exited the old V&A building. He was beaming with pride and anticipation as he walked down the long stone steps. He couldn't wait to hear what else the Magistrum had to say. His life was now assured amongst the top echelons of society.

He turned west and sniffed. Clear. East and he smelt the sweat of the men and the fish from the boats returning to the harbour. At least there would be something decent to eat today. He strode confidently along the rubble paths surrounding the city's corn fields on his way to his sleeping pod. Being a scentirium did have its advantages even if his current job was repetitive but that would soon change. He was glad his family genes had mutated the way they had after the GM epidemic; he wouldn't have survived as a worker with no sense of smell, taste or touch.

Marcus reached the start of the city. Old stone buildings pitted with bullet holes were now linked together by new gate houses and guard posts. He stopped and took a deep breath. Unfamiliar and unexpected scents burnt his nose and awoke the memory banks. His brain quickly assimilated what the smells could be: aviation fuel, cordite, phosphorus and sweat and an unknown sweet grassy smell. In the split second it took Marcus to yell, "Gas attack!", the drones had dropped their canisters. Marcus keeled over. The high pitched squeals made by the canisters on impact instantly disoriented him. A lime green smoke started to drift over the area, sticking in his nose and throat. He sensed rather than heard a figure behind him but he was too faint to fight back as rough hands dragged him into the building.

Marcus coughed and spluttered, spitting out the green dust which had formed thick phlegm in his throat. The room was pitch-black. Marcus scrambled about trying to find the rough hands that had saved him. The floor was cold damp stone. He heard a sharp click and stopped moving as a pale green glow grew to the left of him. In the ghostly light he saw a woman, her brown hair shorn into a workers' crew cut, a black cap shadowing her face from his view. She nodded silently and handed him a small cold metal canister with a mask attachment. He sniffed several times, trying to smell what was happening and where he was but there was nothing. Not even the remnants of the acidic smoke of the fire bombs. A violent cough racked his lungs.

"It's oxygen. Put it on and breathe deeply."

Marcus slumped against the wall. The phlegm was clogging his nose. He placed the mask on and took a deep lung full. No pain, no increased heartbeat. After a few intakes of the gas Marcus felt able to stand. His eyes were becoming accustomed to the gloom and he saw that he was in a small anteroom off a corridor.

"Where are we? Who are you?" Marcus thought he recognised the woman but his eyes were streaming and the effort of those few words caused him to start coughing again.

"Can you walk?" Marcus nodded his reply "Good, then follow me. I'll explain when we are in a safer place. We are still too near the surface."

With that the woman walked swiftly out of the room, taking the light with her. Marcus staggered after her just in time to see her take a right hand turn a few steps down the corridor. The passageway twisted and turned on a slight downward trajectory for what Marcus guessed was about half a mile, passing several doors and archways before they arrived at their destination, a small square door set low into the wall. There were no visible signs of a lock on the front but the woman had placed her hands over what looked like old iron rivets and the door opened slowly.

"Sit," said the woman after they were both safely in the room with the door closed behind them. Marcus couldn't see anywhere to sit until the woman lit a couple of old oil lamps and a warm luminescence flooded the space. The room was square in shape with stone walls covered in deteriorating plaster work and another small door in the opposite corner to the one they had entered. The furniture was sparse, just a bare wooden table with two plain chairs and an armchair covered in red velvet, now worn through, embroidered with flowers in green and pink, the high back topped by a fluted design. The woman left the room.

Marcus moved over and stroked the back of the chair, feeling the smooth roughness of the velvet yield to his touch. He took a deep breath but he smelt nothing. Marcus sank down into the chair. He rocked himself back and forward. Without his sense of smell he was nothing, no talents, no other abilities. He would be forced into becoming a worker, all his privileges gone. Marcus began to weep. The woman returned, pulled over one of the wooden chairs and sat down facing him. She wrapped her hand around his and lifted his face until he was looking straight at her. Her face was scarred, her nose crooked but it was her piercing blue eyes that he thought he recognised. He stared hard but the memory would not rise to the surface.

"Here drink this." She handed Marcus an old chipped tin mug filled with a steaming golden liquid. Instinctively he bent to sniff the contents. The lack of smell started the tears again. "Drink it. It might help your ability come back quicker. The green smoke, it is a virus, like the old common cold. The gas doesn't kill, just debilitates for a few days. We think that the Authority is to blame. Clever really; panic the city and then appear to fight back without ever naming the enemy. But with your nasal passages it will have a different effect. "

Marcus took a small sip. The woman laughed. "I'm not trying to kill you. If I'd wanted to do that I would have just left you out there." She got up from the chair and started to busy herself with dishes on the table.

Marcus wiped the back of his hand across his face, clearing away the tears. "What's in it? It's strange not being able to smell it and tell right away."

"Nettles, honey, some other crushed plants and a shot of whisky. Don't worry…"

Marcus blew on the liquid a few times before gulping it down greedily, his stomach reminding him that it had been hours since he had last eaten. He sighed and sat back in the arm chair. The warmth from the fire and the liquid was making him drowsy. His eyes began to close. Before he succumbed, Marcus thought he heard her voice.

"You sleep now, Marcus. You need it."

Marcus awoke to the sounds of muffled conversations behind him. He didn't want to turn around so he started to yawn and stretch to let them know he was awake. He thought he could smell warm fresh bread for a moment but then the scent was gone. He heard a man's voice saying goodbye. The door they had entered closed and the woman came and stood beside him.

"How are you feeling? You had a good long sleep."

"Not sure. I thought I smelt bread but nothing now. "

"Good. It was bread. Come eat. Hopefully your gift will return soon."

Marcus stood up and moved to the table. The bread was warm and smothered in butter. After a few bites he thought he could taste the creamy milk and the spicy yeast. He stopped chewing.

"Tasting it?"

Marcus nodded slowly.

"Even better. Your sense of smell will return very soon. You may feel like you have a bad hangover for a few days but you weren't exposed enough to the virus for it to do any lasting damage."

Marcus returned to enjoying the bread, a new sense of relief spreading over him. He finished off his meal with another cup of the golden liquid the woman gave him and stretched his legs out under the table.

Small pockets of smells were coming back to him now; the pine wood burning on the fire, the damp cold smell from the plastered wall and the honey and ginger from the drink. He took a deep breath. Scents assaulted his brain. Marcus stared at the women, his memory fighting to bring forward a recollection, cinnamon, seaweed, rain and cotton. He realised that he knew her.

"Elspeth? Elspeth, it is you... But they said you were dead. How? What happened? They said it was an accident." Marcus began to move towards her. Elspeth, his best friend, his only ally against the world, the one who had spent hours helping him build up his memory banks of smells.

Elspeth smiled a thin slow smile and looked at him. "I lost my sense of smell. I was of no use to the Authority anymore."

"But how... why? Could you not have just stayed as a tutor? You were the best."

"It wasn't that simple. I was given an order. I didn't want to be part of it.

94

The Authority saw me as a weakness. A scentirium can't have any weaknesses; you know that. So as a punishment they broke my nose, robbed me of my abilities and condemned me to a life as a worker."

"What order could be so bad?"

Elspeth cocked her head to one side and looked straight at Marcus. "What age are you now? Eighteen? Soon you'll be tested and then given your orders."

"Yes," Marcus replied excitedly. "I turned eighteen last month and the results came back today. I'm pure."

Slowly Elspeth shook her head. "Oh Marcus, I wish that wasn't the case. I wish I could spare you from what is coming next. I had to leave all that I knew and loved. I'd hoped you wouldn't have to make the same choice."

Marcus felt insulted. He was proud to be pure. He stared at Elspeth, his nostrils flaring as he tried to control what he said next. Being a scentirium was all that he knew. Then he remembered the fear he had experienced when his sense of smell had gone and his anger left him. He lowered his gaze and shook his head. Elspeth took hold of his hands again.

"But… but didn't you even miss me?"

"Marcus, I couldn't have stayed. I would have lost my identity. I would have become just another commodity. I didn't want that. Me being able to smell water, food or emotions; it didn't make me better than everybody else, it just made me different. My sense of smell returned eventually but I never told the Authority."

Marcus didn't understand. He had been picked as a scentirium as a child and taken away to the training facility. He didn't know any other life. He was excited to know what the Authority was planning for him. They were his family. Elspeth took Marcus's head; resting it on her shoulder, she stroked his hair. He smelled the warm cotton of her blouse and the faint citrus notes of her skin. Memories of being a frightened little boy in a new sterile dormitory rushed through his head. Elspeth had been his only friend in the facility. They had always been together and comforted each other. As they grew up they had grown closer until the day after her eighteenth birthday she had disappeared without a word. Her scent had lingered around him for weeks and now he could breathe it in again.

Elspeth spoke slowly, barely above a whisper. "I too have full alleles. I would have been used to reproduce other full breeds. The workers are good for the manual labour but they will soon outnumber the pure. So they keep the workers down through attacks like the gas attack and continue with the structured breeding programme."

"No. I don't believe you. The Authority wouldn't do that."

"Yes they do. Why do you think we were raised in the dormitory? We are part of the programme. I didn't want that. If I had a child it would mean no love, no family and no contact with them. Their life would become what ours was – in a facility until they reached eighteen."

"But the Authority looks after us…"

"Yes, you'll get a better job, nicer accommodation and a good food supply. But you will belong only to the Authority. They won't risk anything like emotional decisions damaging their resources. No love, no relationships. Those are the rules. I was offered the same package. That's the order I refused."

Elspeth held him tighter. The room was still. Marcus could hear the fire crackling and feel the warmth of her body against his. Smell filled his senses, hot, warm, comforting, the smell of affection. He breathed deeply, drinking it all in. "I really wished something better for you. I loved you. You do still have a choice." Elspeth paused. "We'd better get you back. I'll come and find you soon. Please think about what I've said. Our genes may have altered but not our humanity."

Marcus was soaked with sweat when he finally woke from his nightmares. The smells from his pores had filled his dreams with images of Elspeth and the dormitory of his childhood. He had tried to remember the smell of his parents, any warmth from an earlier memory but nothing came. He grudgingly accepted what Elspeth said about his past was real.

Marcus showered quickly and dressed for work. He wanted to hear what the Magistrum had to offer but he already knew his answer. Cinnamon, cotton, rain and seaweed would bring him comfort when he desired it.

LOVAGE SOUP

Catherine Maidment

A bright, late June morning, first of the holidays, and Jeanette brought me my coffee in bed.

"I need to tell you something," she said in a shaky voice that made me sit up and pay attention right away.

To my astonishment, Jeanette sat on the edge of the bed, tears channelling her face.

"I've just had it with teaching, Alistair. I'm never going back. Twenty-eight years and now that stupid advisor – who looks like he's never had a class of five-year-olds in his life – tells me I spend too much time teaching the children to read!"

"Surely you don't need to pay much attention to him, do you?"

"Unfortunately, yes. We've got to introduce an 'integrated day'. The kids play all they like and just do reading and number work when they feel like it. It'll never work. I won't go back."

I realised she was serious, probably stressed even more than I was at the end of a difficult term.

"OK," I said. "I'm sure we can cope with just my salary now the kids are away."

Later, when Jeanette was out at the shops, I sat down and worked out our finances. We'd both had enough years of service to guarantee decent pensions when we retired and with only ten years to go, perhaps we could do something more relaxed in the meantime. There must be other ways of making a living. After all, I was pretty fed up with teaching too. It was no fun trying to motivate fourteen-year-old boys to learn French when they could scarcely cope with the English language. Discipline was worse every year. Even thinking about it made me angry and I found I was scratching at a little lump on the side of my face. Warts! That was all I needed. I'd noticed a couple on my fingers too. Perhaps I should see a doctor. Maybe next week.

Jeanette greeted the idea of a change with great excitement.

"It's a chance to do something worthwhile!" she declared.

"Like working as missionaries in Africa?"

"No! Much nearer to home. We could buy a plot of land somewhere and help the environment by growing some food."

Although it sounded quite noble, especially with all this stuff about climate change in the papers nearly every day, I didn't much fancy the 'good life' myself. I imagined digging acres of ground to plant potatoes and perhaps getting up at some ungodly hour to milk a cow. No. Sainsbury's was just fine for my needs.

Jeanette reassured me that all this hard work was unnecessary. We could do our bit by growing stuff to sell and we didn't have to be self-sufficient to make a difference. We could even just plant seeds and sell the young plants to the keen customers who wished to do the rest themselves.

"Look how busy garden centres are every weekend," she enthused. "Everyone wants to get in on this 'grow your own' business. There's a huge demand for young plants."

Early next spring saw us settled in a new bungalow in the Carse of Gowrie. We had a couple of acres of land that we'd had dug over and prepared, and Jeanette was to be found most mornings in a heated potting shed, sowing seeds in trays, pricking out older seedlings and potting them up. I was surprised at how deftly she worked, scarcely noticing the time as she happily beavered away. I felt a bit left out to begin with especially since Jeanette had laughed at me for planting some tulips upside down – how was I supposed to know which way was up? In some kind of role reversal, I spent more of my time in the kitchen, experimenting with Indian, Thai, Chinese and French recipes I researched on the internet. Jeanette seemed to appreciate my efforts when she could finally be persuaded to come inside.

I was also kept occupied with the business side of the venture. As a language teacher, bookkeeping and VAT were alien subjects to me but I'd no alternative but to learn. This I had expected but I'd had no idea just how much legislation and red tape was involved in growing a few plants and selling them to the public. Every day it seemed there was a plethora of government forms and leaflets on our doormat. There were forms to fill in for this, licences to obtain for that. Even for a simple trip to the Farmers' Market with a car boot full of young herbs. Surely all this bureaucracy was unnecessary?

We had inspectors visiting us too, snooping into every corner. I thought I'd seen enough of inspections in the past. Did they think we were growing cannabis or something? Apparently we had to watch out for things like New Zealand flatworms. These invasive creatures could easily be accidentally introduced to the land, being pests by not only eating the native earthworms but by degrading the soil. Our business would be ruined. There was more to this whole venture than potting up a few herbs and selling them to the public. Teaching was not the only stressful occupation! Jeanette, however, seemed happier than I ever remembered her.

Over the first year, business was steady. Some regular customers treated us like friends and inundated us with cuttings and seedlings from their own gardens. Despite my misgivings about flatworms, Jeanette, who scarcely had a minute to spare, would hurriedly plant these donations in a corner of the garden near the bungalow. That area became rather overgrown as some of these new specimens became rank and choked out others.

"It's my wildlife area," Jeanette would say to anyone who remarked on the growing wilderness in the corner.

Then one day, I asked if she had any lovage.

"Lovage?" she asked. "No one is interested in that. It's a rather old-fashioned herb."

"Yes, but apparently it tastes a bit like celery and I've got a great recipe for lovage soup."

"Well, I think there's some in the wild patch, Alistair. I'm a bit busy right now, just get it yourself."

I looked hard at the so-called wild area in disbelief. The plants had spread over the entire corner outside our kitchen. God knew what was growing there. We were due a visit from an inspector next week and if he found any of those invasive species listed in the multitude of leaflets I had to plough through every week, we were in big trouble. Why did Jeanette not take things seriously? I'd told her it was a bad idea to plant anything if she didn't know where it was from. She was just too trusting.

Right! No lovage soup for you today, darling. I grabbed my fork from the shed and began to tackle the patch. Stabbing viciously at the mini wilderness, I felt my pent up frustrations begin to dissolve.

Most of the vegetation came away easily enough, at least as far as the greenery was concerned, and I proudly trundled away three wheelbarrow loads to the compost heap at the far end of the garden. But now the hard work began. Some of this stuff had roots nearly a metre long, spreading sideways as well as downwards through the soil, tenaciously resisting my bare-handed efforts at eradication. Lastly, I dug over the compost heap. I would not put it past that nosy inspector to sniff out unlicensed plants there.

Eventually, scratched, aching and filthy, I staggered to the kitchen door.

Jeanette looked up from her sandwich. "What on earth have you been up to, Alistair? You're filthy and you've got nasty red weals all over your hands and down the side of your face."

"It's making me feel itchy too. Must be something in that so-called wild patch. I've cleared it out. The inspectors are coming and we can't risk them condemning us for God knows what's growing there."

After a long relaxing bath, I felt better. The scratches were stinging a bit from the hot water but the itchiness had gone. Then I noticed something odd in the mirror. That little lump on the side of my face had disappeared. I couldn't even feel where it had been. The warts on my hands had gone too. Even more amazing, on examining my feet the swelling on my big toe joint – a bunion I was sure – had also vanished.

Smiling to myself, I decided that I'd investigate the contents of the compost heap after the inspector had called. We might yet find an easy way to fund a luxurious retirement.

A LOVELY DAY FOR AN AIRSTRIKE

C.B. Donald

'I have wanted to, and have been, documenting those characters that are disappearing — hermits and such — because nowadays everyone is the same.'

Ragnar Axelsson

Standing on the edge of the lake Siggi stares ahead into the fading dark of the pre-dawn. The rocks in his pocket weigh him down. The wind is cold and whips his thinning hair on to his face. He wonders how he came to be here. He concentrates and thinks back.

Siggi is half asleep as he heads to the gym. There are only a few people in there. Some tacky chart hit is blaring from the video screen, all bass and electronics. It's a parody of a song he'd heard way back. Parody hits are all the rage now, he understands. Trying to block it out, he sits down on the bike and punches in his routine. There are a couple of jocks pressing weights three or four metres away, mindlessly jabbering about football. Fram in the Euro Cup it seems, beating some Italian cracks. Can that be true?

He thinks back to his first football game, a good half a century back, to see Fram. His granddad's team, they'd been the best team in Reykjavik but had fallen in stature and were now regularly behind their rivals. But they were granddad's team, whether good or bad. On that day, a crowd of a couple of hundred Fram fans in some Euro first round game. A warm day in July, cirrus strands picked out against the blue high above. Were the opposition Finnish or Faroese? He gets the solid feel of his granddad's craggy hand around his while patiently explaining the rules of the game and which player is which.

"Siggi, that's the goalie, Johansson. His job is to keep the ball out of the goal."

"Does he manage?"

"Sometimes he does. Let's hope he will today, eh?"

He remembers Johansson well. A flash in his mind of the keeper stretching to save a penalty in a league game against Valur. But they lost 2-1 anyway. How can fate let him recall instants and facts like that so vividly but sometimes strip away what he did for a living, or what he had for breakfast?

This hopelessness makes his mind up. He decides it's time to enact the plan he's been hoarding all these years. Now is the time for the fight-back. Before his mind completely fails him.

Half in a daze he goes home. He picks up the bomb and drives to the Parliament building. He knows a secret place in the air vents from when Baldir once worked there. Who'd suspect an old codger like him? He sets it up – no hitch at all – then mails the media networks his letter. He times it to ensure maximum damage. Population reduction is a start. He has no illusions he can save Reykjavik – that fight had been lost long ago – but it's a good way to start a revolution. Perhaps his rallying cry will ignite a movement.

He drives out of the city. Down the south road, passing the dead filling station that has been subsumed by sprawl. What was that poem about the death of a filling station? He should be able to remember that one, for Christ's sake. He had read it at Baldir's funeral after all.

This used to be the edge of the city; now he still has a few miles to go. Hallsgrimskirkja's volcanic-styled tip is just about visible in his rear mirror, far behind. He tries not to squint at the big park on the right side that was eaten by housing projects some twenty years back. He and Baldir had been at the forefront of Reykjavik's preservation movement. For all the good it had done them. Or the city for that matter. Housing was too important to growth, after all. He gets an image of the fat mayor's fat smirking face announcing the verdict. A shudder. It comes back that the mayor went on to be Prime Minister, king of Iceland's 'Golden Age', 'The Man Harnessing the Nordic Tiger'. All that shit didn't do much for him then and still makes him queasy even now. They'll get theirs. They and all like them.

He heads out past the new sections of town, trying to imagine it all as it used to be before the hundreds and thousands swarmed here to get those jobs. He gets to the Hispanic section, and, after that, Halal warehouses. It isn't Reykjavik at all. Not *his* Reykjavik anyway. Eventually, the houses thin out and he's in the wastelands heading east where he can convince himself it's like old times. He drives further. He parks beside the lake and listens to old CDs until he drifts to sleep. And he doesn't dream at all.

Standing on the edge of the lake he stares ahead into the fading dark of the pre-dawn. The rocks in his pocket weigh him down. The wind is cold and whips his thinning hair on to his face. He's getting to the nub of what led him here now and his brain throbs. He thinks back to the evening before and gets an image of his walk home. The neon is garish, and it almost blinds him. 'Fish' it says, like it's a novelty, like every frigging restaurant in the city doesn't stock it. A crowd of young people are sharing a joke loudly on the kerb. A spiky-haired man, maybe twenty, is laughing so hard he's wiping tears from his eyes. A purple rain-coated girl opposite him has her glasses in her left hand, rocking with mirth. He gets closer and sees they're watching some portable video screen of some guy falling off a skateboard. Does this pass for entertainment these days?

He suddenly becomes hyper-aware of all his surroundings. He sees the jammed streets are full of laughing faces like those ones: lovers walking hand in hand; a family leaving a cinema, jabbering with excitement about a movie they've just seen; and a street juggler with a clapping crowd round her. These people don't care what his town used to be like, have no idea what they've lost. They carry on and thrive in the new city he hates so much. Throwing himself into the lake would be what? Futile? Something beyond that.

Beyond that. He has another memory lurching in his mind: his grandfather, smelling of fish-oil and cloves, in that damp kitchen at Vogar, reading the paper and grumbling about the radio.

"Call that shit music? He's just whining, not singing. Garbage, boy, garbage." Granddad hadn't looked up once.

He'd been hurt then and thinking of it now brought the ghost of the agony back. It was his favourite song. That granddad could dismiss it so casually was painful. But then how had he reacted to the sheep's head?

"Ugh! You eat that granddad? Really? Why? Are you crazy?" Was he any better than today's kids with their lack of respect for what has gone before?

With a jarring clarity it comes to him that he hadn't planted the bomb at all. He's getting confused between his dreams and his waking life. The specialist said that this would happen more and more as time went by, even if he remembered to take the meds. And he has no idea if he has taken them. Memory is what he has to hold on to, but even that is blurring, like the mist on the morning lake. He can never be sure where the horizon ends and where the water begins now. Will there be a time when he'll forget what he has lost? Perhaps that is something worth living for after all. Can he still remember the old poem about the filling station? He knows intuitively that it holds some message for him. He concentrates extra hard to see if he can grab it from the hidden parts of his brain and this time it comes in a clear stream.

Fuel Stop

You are boarded up on the city's edge,
pumps outcompeted and abandoned.
You sold the past –
now you, in turn, are done.
With millions of years of depression you
will transmute by some colossal alchemy
to fuel a future craft
that queues impatiently
at another doomed station.

It never made sense to him when he first heard it but clicks into place now. We are all doomed to be part of the half-remembered past as the future builds upon us. Is that so bad?

Siggi gets back in his car and heads off to get a nice breakfast at his favourite old town restaurant. It's going to be a beautiful day. Who knows how many more of these sunrises he will be able to appreciate?

THE CAT AND THE CORN

J. Stirling

I peered through the dirty glass at the approaching station, trying to keep my balance with one hand supporting my bulging rucksack. As the doors hissed open I emerged from the air-conditioned bliss of the carriage into the unexpectedly scorching glare of high summer in Fife.

I had been anxious that I might not recognise my uncle, Charles. After all I had only been twelve when he last visited my parents but I needn't have worried. His black Jaguar was idling in the disabled bay, its horn honking impatiently to the irritation of everyone in the station. I manhandled my baggage with difficulty through the exit as quickly as I could given my convalescent state and hauled it onto the back seat.

"That's the trouble with Britain today," Charles harrumphed. "Work-shy, the lot of them! All of them on benefits claiming there's no jobs and yet what do you find? Not a single porter! In Kenya there are so many of the blighters you have to beat them off with a stick. Anyway, good journey?"

The sun glinted off the chrome jaguar on the bonnet as we swept out of the station and I remarked on the glorious weather.

Charles nodded. "Bit of a heat-wave. No rain for the past three weeks. Not usually like this though. Anyway, dashed good of you to keep an eye on Balcullen for me, my boy. Couldn't run the risk of leaving the house unoccupied for months on end. Probably come back to find a pack of ruddy gypsies had moved in in my absence, what?"

"No need to thank me," I replied. "It'll be a great opportunity to get on with writing up my Anthropology thesis. I've had to put my degree on hold for a year thanks to the malaria I picked up in India but I'm looking forward to doing a bit of walking and building up my strength."

"Good, good," said Charles. "There's not much else for a young chap to do round here. The nearest town is Aberflisk – ghastly little place. One shop. One pub. Full of inbred peasants… only two surnames in the whole place. It's hardly evolved since the dark ages. Locals still hanging onto their ungodly folk traditions."

"Oh?" I was intrigued.

"Oh, May Day celebrations, scarecrow festivals, that sort of thing. And there's an iron age hill figure overlooking the town. When I passed through yesterday they'd set it alight again. Some sort of pagan ritual."

"I'd be really interested in seeing it," I said.

"**Be** warned. They're not too friendly to outsiders... always threatening to put the evil eye on you and spreading rumours about big cat sightings. Stuff and nonsense dreamt up by the feeble-minded."

After ten miles we swerved off the main road onto a single-track country lane which twisted up the hill past fields of grazing sheep. Presently we turned right and drove a short distance between hedgerows before scrunching to a halt on the gravel beside an old stone manor house.

"Well, home sweet home and all that. Grab your kit and I'll give you the grand tour," Charles called over his shoulder.

As I got out of the car I was once again taken aback by the ferocity of the afternoon sun and wished I'd thought to bring a hat of some sort. The house was thankfully much cooler. Charles led the way around the bedrooms, bathrooms and kitchen before showing me into a sumptuously furnished drawing room. Large French windows looked out onto an attractive patio and beyond this the lawn spread out like a chenille tablecloth. Stretched out in all directions were low, gently rounded hills, some cultivated, some fluorescent with gorse.

"It's a magnificent view," I exhaled.

"Excellent for wildlife," Charles agreed. "You can sit out here in the evenings and see badgers, roe deer and tawny owls close up. I keep the shotgun handy above the fireplace. If you look over there to the North – that line of trees is the start of Aberflisk woods. You can climb over the stile and follow the track down through the trees to the town. Only a couple of miles."

We returned to the kitchen where Charles got busy fixing dinner. Ten minutes later we were sitting down to a meal of blackened sausages, toast and eggs.

"So tell me, what were you doing in India?" asked Charles.

"I was out researching tribal rituals in Rajasthan for my final year thesis," I replied.

"Odd bunch, the Indians. All sacred cows and monkey gods."

I nodded. "I used to find it strange too but once I'd immersed myself in the culture I realised the beliefs and rituals I'd originally found so bizarre were pretty logical. In fact it made me question much of how we live our lives in the west."

"Not sure what you mean, dear boy."

"Well, things like our endless desire for the latest technology or our vast consumption of meat or the loss of our extended kinship groups to name just a few. Perhaps we would be happier if we took a step back and led simpler lives."

"Steady on! Sounds as if you're in danger of going native! Chap I knew in Zambia did that. Ended up living in a mud hut. Quite embarrassing."

Our conversation was interrupted by the ringing of the telephone in the hall. A few minutes later Charles returned to the kitchen with glee radiating from his jowls.

"Just had some excellent news! I've finally managed to put a stop to the Aberflisk wind turbine!"

I looked at him quizzically and he went on to explain. "The community action group – or the Aberflisk Mafia as I call them – had planned to stick a ruddy great turbine above the town. I would have been able to see the rotating tips of the monster from the windows in the attic. They were claiming it would provide free power for the community but you can bet they only wanted to do it because someone was going to get very rich out of the deal."

Charles popped the last piece of toast in his mouth and continued. "Anyway, now that you're here and that's sorted there's no need for me to stick around any longer. There are some flights south I could catch tonight, spend a few days in my club in London before heading out to Nairobi or Dar Es Salaam or wherever takes my fancy."

"How long are you planning to be away?" I asked.

"Hard to say as yet but I won't be back before Easter. British weather and all that. And as long as you're keeping an eye on this place there's no need for me to hurry back, what?"

"I'm only too happy to stay as long as I can," I assured him.

"Well then, let me get my kit together, then what say we drive down to Aberflisk in the Jag for a quick drink. Let you see the place. Then I'll carry on to the airport and you can walk back through the woods at your leisure."

The short drive took us past ripe cornfields and as we rounded a corner I got my first glimpse of Aberflisk. The town consisted of one long main street overlooked by an extensive semi-circle of hillside which formed the green canvas for a large black smouldering figure of a cat framed by the surrounding Aberflisk woods.

Charles said, "I'll park while you go and get the drinks in."

Despite being early evening, the air was hotter than ever. The grey smoke from the burning on the hill rested like a heavy eiderdown over the town sealing in the heat. It sapped my strength and my limbs felt leaden. The street was deserted save for one bony cat which stared at me unflinchingly from a low windowsill. The acrid smell of smoke caught at the back of my throat and there was a sense of malice in the air. I needed a drink.

I turned my attention to the pub. An intricately woven wreath of corn stalks hung around a sign which read 'The Reaper'. I squared my shoulders and opened the door.

I could smell the cloying sweetness of stale beer and hear the chatter and clinking of glass on glass typical of most village pubs. Old men played dominoes in the corner tables while the younger patrons stood in clusters next to the bar. Other than the barmaid, who smiled at me in welcome, no one gave me a second glance.

The tension in my shoulders eased as I approached her. "A pint of lager for me, please, and a scotch on the rocks for my... ah... landlord. He's just coming."

"Coming right up," she said as she reached for the glasses. "And do feel free to help yourself to some Lammas bread."

"Oh? What's Lammas bread?" I asked.

She indicated a large platter of thickly-sliced crusty bread spread generously with butter.

"Today's the first of August. Lammas Day. Traditionally this is the first day of the harvest and the bread's made from the first cut of the corn. Today's the day you reap what you have sown."

"Thank you. It looks delicious," I said as I took a slice. "It's great to find somewhere that still keeps up the old customs."

"There's a Lammas March through the town later this evening. You should stick around, it's all good..."

But her sentence was cut short and the room fell silent as all eyes turned to glare at Charles. He strode into the room oblivious to the hostility. I hastily motioned him to follow me out the side door to the beer garden where it might be quieter. From this vantage point I could see a rich patchwork of allotments embroidered with vegetable plots and studded with fruit trees running down from the back of the houses. I could see the fat bees which droned in and out of their wooden hives and beyond them the lazy river drifting without haste towards the North Sea.

Charles was pensive as he surveyed the scene. "I was just thinking how perfect it is," he said as he sipped his scotch. "A friend I'm hoping to meet in Nairobi asked me to keep my eyes open for a suitable site for a plastics factory he's hoping to set up in Scotland."

I choked on my beer all too aware that Charles's booming voice carried easily to the drinkers at neighbouring tables. "I think there would be considerable opposition to that," I spluttered.

Charles was dismissive. "No need to worry about that. I'm not without influence, dear boy."

The oppressive heat of the day met with the rising hot tide of embarrassment. I could feel the T-shirt sticking to my back and my temples were thumping. I pressed my glass to my forehead.

Charles glanced at the gold Rolex on his wrist, downed the last gulp of his whisky and got to his feet. "Right, time I was off. Flight to catch and all that. See you next year some time."

And I was left alone as the sun dipped below the horizon. I finished the last dregs of my beer and made my way to the gents. Even my eyeballs felt hot and I splashed cold water over my face for some momentary relief. When I came out I found that the pub was empty. The thump, thump, thump was more intense now and I could feel it resonating through my chest. And then I realised that it was in fact the rhythmic booming of a bass drum out in the street. The Lammas March had begun.

I stepped outside to find a sea of masked spectators filling the pavement in excited expectation as the march approached. At its head, a figure dressed in a white Elvis jump suit topped with a wolf-man mask danced, whirled and sporadically lunged into the crowd brandishing his flaming torch, to the squealing delight of the children.

As the main body of the procession drew closer the increasing volume of the drumbeat, which was now accompanied by the keening wail of a dozen vuvuzelas, did nothing to help my splitting headache and I began to feel nauseous. More grotesque, gyrating creatures dressed in onezies and a bizarre assortment of plastic masks passed in front of me. Then came a bishop on a mobility scooter leading a phalanx of hooded monks armed with pitchforks. Behind them a huge white Clydesdale horse clopped stoically on its massive hooves in the midst of the fracas. Its bridle, mane and tail were decorated with pleated corn stalks but it was the rider who held my attention. He was clad in a long white robe and his face was hidden behind a blank mask. There was an awkwardness about this figure which unsettled me. I noticed his hands gripping the pommel, the way he leaned too far back in the saddle and his crooked deformed legs. As he drew alongside I saw a second mask on the back of his head and it dawned on me that he was seated backwards on his mount – symbolic of the past and the future.

THE CAT AND THE CORN

The throng surged behind the horse and I found myself carried along in the tide, and still the drum crashed and the vuvuzelas blared. I was buffeted and jostled in a sea of jubilant revellers as the march turned up a narrow lane which led to the hillside. Hemmed in by the mob, gasping for breath and blinded by sweat I was drowning in a medieval depiction of Hell – only in place of gargoyles' heads were the plastic faces of Donald Duck and Margaret Thatcher.

I was trembling as the pressure finally eased and we spilled out onto the smouldering cat. The horse came to a halt and the crowd fanned out around it. There was an immediate hush as the bishop raised his hand.

"Reap what you sow!"

At his cry the monks surrounded the horse and tried to unseat the rider but he twisted and kicked out at them and I saw that his hands had been bound behind his back. This man was no willing participant and what had until now seemed just bewildering and uncomfortable now felt deeply sinister. With my naked face I felt all too visible... and vulnerable. On unsteady legs I eased myself to the back of the rabble and noticed there were only about twenty yards of hillside between me and the dark woods which lead back to Balcullen.

The mob began to chant "Reap what you sow! Reap what you sow! Reap what you sow!" louder and faster as the monks wrestled the man from the saddle. As the anticipation grew I could feel the bile rising inside me yet I was unable to tear my eyes from the struggling man in white. The atmosphere was at fever pitch when a flashing blade of lightning sliced overhead and I saw behind the mask Charles's desperate eyes locked onto mine.

In that split second I was torn between the urge to rush to his aid and the equally powerful instinct of self-preservation. An almighty explosion of thunder brought me to my senses and I turned and ran. I raced across the clearing as heavy raindrops began to pelt down plastering my clothes to my body, slicking down my hair. A shout rang out but I didn't dare turn my head to see how many were in pursuit. The rubber soles of my shoes began to slip on the now sodden grass and in my peripheral vision I saw monks with pitchforks gaining on me. I was almost at the trees. One final burst of energy was all I needed. But my foot skidded. As I tumbled forward lightning illuminated the hillside and in slow motion I saw I was falling not three yards from the bared teeth of a great black panther. My knees crumpled and the palms of my hands slammed down into the mud as the cat twitched its tail and made ready to pounce. My head crashed to the ground and all I remember was two monks screaming headlong towards the beast, driving it back into the darkness.

When I came to I was lying on a narrow bed under cool sheets. I was in a room I did not recognise but through the flimsy curtains I could see daylight. Although my limbs ached, my head felt clear. There was a short double-knock then the door clicked open and the barmaid from last night stood before me carrying a tray.

"I'm glad to see you're awake at last," she smiled setting the tray down on the bedside cabinet. "I'm Caroline, by the way."

"Where am I?"

"In a guest room above The Reaper. We brought you up here last night when you collapsed in the bar. You had a raging fever. The doctor said it was best to keep you here till it broke. How are you feeling now?"

I felt thirsty. Confused images flitted through my mind: jaguars, pitchforks, flaming torches swam before my eyes… and Charles.

"Charles?" my dry tongue stuck to the roof of my mouth.

"He was worried about you but when we assured him we'd look after you he went on his way. Said he'd send you a postcard. You're welcome to stay here as long as you wish or I can give you a lift back anytime if you feel you can manage on your own."

Nothing made any sense. But then I remembered I had felt like this once before – it was the day I had woken up in a hospital in Jaipur. I breathed more evenly.

After eating a light breakfast I went outside to wait for Caroline to bring the car round. The air was sweet and cool. Children were playing with skateboards while teenagers flirted in the bus shelter. It was a beautiful, crisp summer morning and the little town seemed washed clean by the rain. As I watched Caroline draw up to the kerb I felt happy. The next ten months were full of promise. But as I opened the car door an elderly man trundled past on a mobility scooter and I saw that mounted on the front of his steering column was a chrome jaguar.

FEEDING TIME

Ann-Marie Aslen

– Da…ad, I need some help with ma homework.

– If it's maths again you're on your own. Ask mum.

– It's History. An' ah'm confused.

– Hand it over then. I used to be a dab hand at history. What are you studying? Vikings? Columbus? World War 1? Not the bloody Battle of Hastings, is it?

– Nah, it's the Great Collapse. I jist dont get it.

– Oh. Well, what bit don't you get?

– EVERYTHING! Like, whit wuz it? Whit caused it? How'd we survive?

– Okay, this is going to be a long night so shut up and open your ears. Mind, I was only a bit older than you at the time so I don't really know everything that caused it.

– Ye know mair thon me. Ah'm listenin, ah'm listenin!

– Right. Well, did you study Western society yet?

– Aye. Whit aboot it?

– Did you understand it? It was a lot different to the society we have now. You need to try and understand what it was like back then.

– Weel, they hud bits o paper an plastic an they could get stuff wi it. But it wasnae real paper, jist pretend? Nae like now, everybudy has a hoose an aw, an if ye want stuff like a telly ye jist get an auld een that naebody's usin or trade or work fer a new one. Folk didnae hae a hoose wi'oot bits o paper or plastic.

– Not quite. God, this will take ages. Right, the paper was called 'money' and was used in place of barter. You could keep the money you earned in a bank. The bank would loan you money to buy stuff and you paid them back with some extra on top.

– Why?

– To thank them for loaning you the money, I suppose.

– Why? It wisnae their money they were loanin. Folk should've jist borrowed fae their pals and nivver minded the banks.

– I never really understood that bit myself. Anyway, the problem was, banks started lending money that didn't exist yet.

– You wot?

– They were lending money people hadn't paid back yet. Eventually there was a small bank crash in 2008 when the banks lost everyone's money and everybody in the world had to give the banks all their money just so they could keep working and buying stuff. Cos without the banks they couldn't.

– That wis stupid. The banks could've lost that an aw.

– Well, six years later in 2014 they did. That was the start of the Great Collapse. Without money people couldn't buy food or heat their homes, or pay for doctors and stuff. The rich people paid mercenaries called police to protect them from poor people looking for food. Entire countries ended up in civil war. Finally armies kept people in order and everybody got a ration card for food and stuff. That wasn't the worst bit though.

– Seriously? Ah'd a thought civil war wis bad enough.

– No. See, in order to get more money than everybody else, companies and seriously rich people were polluting the environment and destroying natural resources like there was no tomorrow. The climate started changing in response to all this pollution. Storms got worse, droughts affected places that usually got rain, flooding destroyed coastlines, landslides carried away towns, hurricanes destroyed islands.

– Is that why we a live high up on hills an stuff? An why maist o thon big cities are under the water? Oor biology teacher took us on a trip tae Lunnon. We seen fish an aw sorts swimmin in a big palace. It wis braw.

– That was London, you muppet. And the palace was Westminster Cathedral. Never saw them myself.

– So, wis that the Great Collapse?

– Nope, but it caused it. You see, thousands of people died in the natural disasters but worse was the droughts. Crops died and people started to starve. Sources of clean water got fewer as some countries refused to stop their factories polluting everything just so they could keep making stuff no-one wanted or really needed for trading with. Some companies tried to make crops that could grow in drought areas but war broke out before they knew if they'd grow or not.

– The Water War!

– Also called World War Three, or the shortest war in history. America, China and Russia started invading other countries to steal their water but without money to buy oil their machines ground to a halt. Oil-producing countries were starving to death and stopped making oil. Within five weeks the war was over, for all the good it did. All they'd managed to do was destroy some of the few fertile grounds there were. World-wide starvation erupted. Millions were migrating, eating everything in their path, plant and animal. That's why we lost all the whales and most of the fish species. Not to mention all the tigers, lions, elephants, rhinos, dogs, cats, nearly every kind of animal but insects and stuff too fast to be caught like monkeys.

– We saw pictures o them in books. Ah wid've liked to've seen a tiger. They looked braw.

– Well, that was the Great Collapse. Civilisation in every country just collapsed all at once. It was every man for himself, brutal fighting for a tin of beans, the rich

114

hoarding what they could and using it to pay for protection. People traded whatever they could for something to eat, diamond necklaces, computers, mobiles… For a while it seemed like everyone was going to die, humans becoming extinct.

– You lived through that, didn't ye da? Wis it really bad?

– It was. Remember the family photo I showed you?

– The one wi you an auntie Susie an uncle Adam an yer cousins? Aye.

– I'm the only one in my family who survived the Great Famine in Britain. I suppose we were lucky, being an island. Very few people thought to cross over to look for food. It was estimated that the world's population of eight billion dropped by a third in just a year. Plus we had floods and storms to survive as well. And tornados. I nearly shit myself when one landed near Manchester and ripped apart the shanty town I was living in. They were finding corrugated iron and bodies miles away. That's when I decided to come to Scotland. They were surviving better than in England. Lots of hills to escape the flash floods and places to grow potatoes. I hate potatoes.

– Me an' aw. Mam loves them tho. So whit happened? How'd we survive? Mrs Simmons said there wiz only five hunner million o us left in the whole wurld. Did everybudy else die?

– Nearly. We were in a seriously bad way when *they* came.

– The aliens! They helped us, din't they, da? Mrs Simmons didnae say much aboot them 'cept they'd been through somethin like it on their wurld an had answers.

– In a way. They couldn't help with the climate problems but they showed us how to live with what we had. They certainly solved our overpopulation and starvation problems though!

– How? An why dis Mrs Simmons nae want them back here?

– Well, the aliens made everyone stop fighting and then held a lottery. If your number came up you went to the alien camp. They took about four-fifths of the

FEEDING TIME

world's population. They made sure to leave all the young healthy people though; the potential breeders if you will. And no-one alive then EVER wants the aliens to come back!

– But why? How did that solve overpopulation, da? Whit did the aliens dae wi a them people?

– They ate them.

GOOD NEIGHBOURS

Linda Louden

She looked in disgust at the cloudless sky. It had been a decade of long hot summers, each one longer and hotter than the previous one. It was getting more and more difficult to cultivate her prize flowers, especially since the hosepipe ban had become year round.

Climate change had been playing havoc with the growing competitions in the village for the last few years; it had been a while since she had seen a record breaking marrow, or a decent carrot. Hearing the familiar 'whup, whup, whup', she looked up again. A dark shape in the sky confirmed the spotter chopper. Fools, she thought; no gardener worth her salt would be out watering plants with the sun at its zenith.

She looked over the fence at Ethel's flowers, full of life and colour. How? The old biddy couldn't carry a cup of tea five feet without spilling most of it into the saucer, so she obviously wasn't carting buckets of water up and down the garden; and never a sight of her out with a hose, otherwise Doreen would have found it her painful duty to call the Hosepipe Hotline, the number of which she kept handy in her pinny pocket.

Doreen was looking gloomily at her poor limp Sweet Peas, named for her favourite celebrity, when she heard George's voice floating down from the upstairs window. "She just went out the front door, pet, got that trolley thingy so she will be gone for a while." He had been on sentry duty since 9am, looking for any sign of the enemy.

"Very good. Step down George, and get the kettle on. I'm as parched as me Terry Wogans." She threw another sorrowful look at her pitiful blooms.

Once indoors, the strategy meeting was planned over weak tea and Bath Olivers.

"I'll take the watch this time George; I'd never manage to scale that fence. Put your old corduroys on. I don't want you ripping those slacks."

"OK, pet. This is a bit of excitement, isn't it? I feel a bit like James Bond."

"Humph, just don't expect me to start acting like that Pussy Galore."

Doreen had given up all that malarkey after Michael was born.

George's shudder registered on the Richter scale as his imagination went into overdrive.

"Mind," carried on Doreen seamlessly, "Ethel could be a Rosa Klebb."

"Yeesh!" The thought of Ethel rushing him with spikey shoes caused George a modest aftershock. "Let's get this bloody thing over with." He headed for the garden door.

"Corduroys, George!"

Mid-stride George huffed as he changed direction and headed for the utility room where he was allowed to keep his allotment clothes. Not that he went up there much these days. He was no longer able to grow the root vegetables that he had been so proud of, and the salad vegetables which thrived in the new drier climate were not really his cup of tea. Plus it wasn't the same with Doreen in tow, keen to make it 'together time'. Flippin 'together time'! What happened to his 'peace and quiet time'?

Oh, she was alright was Doreen; he was quite fond of the old gal really. She talked incessantly, but show him a woman who didn't; and at least she was nothing like that Pauline John had married. Talk about change the minute the ring was on her finger! Well, now it was through John's nose and had been for half a century. Or that bloody Ethel next door. Nagged her Harry into his grave, faded away to nothing poor oul bugger. If his coffin had been made of balsa wood they'd have had to have tethered it.

He grunted as he struggled into his corduroys. This hip was getting worse. He kept quiet about it or Doreen would be keeping an even closer eye on him, and his occasional jollies to the bookies and the pub would be curtailed. God alone knew how he was meant to climb that bloody fence!

As she heard the back door close, Doreen turned again to her post at the front window. Mrs Mackie over the road could do with cleaning her nets, she noted, and that front garden – well! You would think the woman had no self-respect at all. She now had two new hips, so absolutely no excuse. She should be offering to do everyone else's.

Only the Good Lord knew how Doreen suffered. She didn't make a song and dance about it – not that she could dance. Not with her hips and knees, housewife's elbow, and stiff neck. Hard neck, George called it, which was probably even more serious.

That cat was on the prowl; he hadn't done its business in her garden since she'd thrown that bucket of washing-up water all over it. The Smiths dog was howling, again. That family was as common as their name; ought never to have been allowed to move into the cul-de-sac. They had been 'of a certain class' up until the Smiths. Now it was 'Chardonnay this' and 'Romeo that' screeched out at all hours.

Norman was glumly polishing his old Ford. Shame he was only legally allowed to drive it on Sundays, but then if he was unwilling to drive an electric or even a hybrid what could he expect? Doreen noticed that another lawn had been lifted and gravelled. She was sad but understood. If these summers continued, she might have to think of doing the same. She had noticed George struggling with the watering can of late.

In the back garden, meanwhile, George had upended the wheelbarrow and wedged an upside down bucket in the spars. Hopefully this would get him over the fence, though God knows how he'd get back. Looking around, he gingerly started his ascent. The bucket wobbled precariously as he lifted his right leg, and as his weight shifted it shot out from under his left. He slammed onto the fence before tumbling over into Ethel's garden clutching his groin. Breath came back, eventually, and the pain subsided to merely excruciating within a few minutes. He staggered to his feet, barely acknowledging the sludge he was standing in, and hobbled onto the lawn. Able finally to stand upright, he looked around in awe.

The lawn he was standing on was slightly spongy, and was a lovely lush shade of green, the envy of any gardener. He noticed the mess where he had fallen, deep footprints and scattered rich brown earth. He peered across at his own pitiful patch; the lawn a variety of browns and yellows, earth like concrete, the flowers wilting or dead.

He looked back at the piece of paradise upon which he had landed. And looked and looked. And then looked closer. In the lawn and flower beds he noticed small spikes of silver. Bending, he realised what they might be and seeking confirmation finally noticed the hose attached to the outside tap and disappearing into the ground.

Well, well! That's how she had done it! He thought back to earlier in the spring. The old biddy had been so keen to know all about their upcoming cruise. Of course, Doreen being Doreen, was more than happy to gloat over the detail of the flight out, where they would be visiting, how long they would be away. Bloody Ethel had even offered (for the first time in thirty years) to take a spare key and water the houseplants, move the post and generally keep an eye open to save his brother John having to come across town.

George even remembered bringing her back a bottle of sweet sherry as a thank you. Devious old bat! He almost had to tip his hat to her, making sure that she had time to get the work done and everything back in place before their return. Her neighbour on the other side was Shane Smith and his brood, so George could guess who Ethel would have paid cash-in-hand to do the work. Problem now was, what to do about it and what to tell Doreen?

She stood in the garden looking at the cloudless sky. This summer was lasting for ever.

"Come and sit down pet, your lemonade is getting warm."

Before she joined George on the deckchairs, she looked around the garden with pride. It had not taken long for everything to pick up once it was getting a regular drink. Looking at her Terry Wogans she regretfully acknowledged that it was probably too late for this year's show, but next year she would wipe the floor.

Sitting down she tilted her glass in the direction of Ethel's house. Blackmail was a dirty word, but it was very nice of the old dear to offer to pay for them to have an underground irrigation system in their garden just like hers!

SNOW

Hamish McBride

Here is the six o'clock news on Wednesday the first of January. The Headlines. Severe weather conditions have led to serious disruption of traffic and communication up and down the country. Many rural roads and rail lines are blocked. The main road and rail routes are open.

Wednesday, first of January. This is my lovely new diary; I'm going to write in it once a week, because last year I tried every day, and the diary entries were boring! Granny gave it to me for Christmas.

My name is Alison Fraser and I stay in Balinrigh, near Inverness, with Mum and Dad, and wee Bobby. Balinrigh has only a few houses and crofts, but still has a Hall where all the local things happen. We were at the Hall last night for New Year's Eve. It wasn't as good as usual because the band couldn't get here. Gren and Peter have both gone sideways in the road at the hill so the county men can't get the ploughs up to clear our roads. My Dad has been taking his digger with a wooden board attached to clear our roads. I watched him put the wood on. I didn't think it would work, but it does. Dad's like that. He can make things work all right.

At the Hall, Dieter and he had a row! I didn't like seeing Dad get angry. He gets red in the face and does swear words. Dieter had asked him to clear his road, which is long and uphill, going to nowhere else. Dad said that he had far too much to do with the lower roads, and didn't have time. Dieter offered Dad money, and that made him angrier. They both were swearing, and Dieter sounded more German than usual. 'Keep your bl----y money,' Dad said, even though we don't have very much.

The snow started on Christmas Eve and was great fun to start with. We had sledging and snowmen and snowballs. The snow hasn't stopped though. Now the snow is higher than me! When we go up our road, I have to jump up to see up the hill! Sam, who is building in the schoolhouse, has put a wood-burning stove into the Hall, so that it can be warm if the electricity is broken. Dad said that some lines were down in other places, and the men can't get there to sort them. He's going to put our spare genny up to the Hall this week, just in case.

SNOW

Granny in Edinburgh phones to ask how we are. She and Gramps can get about by walking, but the cars can't go on the roads. They have to walk to the Moncreiffs for their bridge. Dad says that they would probably walk a long way for bridge!

Here is the six o'clock news on Wednesday, the eighth of January. The Headlines. Britain is still paralyzed by the severe weather. This is the longest cold spell since records began. All the roads between England, Wales and Scotland are blocked. The Government has declared a state of emergency, and the Army is to help with road clearing and with supplies to areas cut off by snow. All military and civilian helicopters have been requisitioned for food delivery. Millions of pounds have been lost from the stock market.

It's the eighth of January. We've had more and more snow. Dad went to measure it and there's ten feet in the field. He had to use his digger and a long trunk of wood to measure it. He and Sam went shopping on Monday. Usually it's the mums who go shopping but Dad and Sam had to borrow the estate skidoo. Dad put runners on an old trailer for the skidoo to pull. They couldn't go by road cause that's blocked, so they went by the old drove road on the ridge down to Inverness. They had lots of work to do! They got to the town but had to leave the skidoo and walk. Dad said that there was just enough room to go one after the other. They got lots of basics; flour for bread and baking, sugar, veg, pasta, tatties, things like that. They couldn't stick to their list, cause the Co-op had lots of empty shelves. They went to Chippies, where Dad meets his wood-cutting friends. The men there say that they have fishermen friends who will bring food up from Edinburgh in their boats cause the cars and lorries can't get through. There's a shed they will use as a warehouse. Dad says the men at Chippies are better at getting things done than the Government!

We've started School at the Hall! Of course I can't get to proper school, so the Mums, and a few Dads, are to teach us. It's funny cause your teachers are also people you know. Jean Munro does English, and she's great. I didn't realise she knew so much. Sam and sometimes Emma do Maths and they are more interesting than Mrs Smith in proper school! That's not hard, anyway! Dieter does German, and I'm not sure about that. I'm scared of him getting angry again, like he did with Dad. He and his family are staying in the Hall. Their Electricity did break, with the line down near the Loch, so they couldn't stay there. Mum bakes bread every day in our house, and is teaching Gert, that's Dieter's wife, to make more bread at the Hall.

Dad and Sam are to do more shopping this week. The Mums have made lists of what they have in their freezers so it can be shared out. Dad and the keeper go out and shoot deer, and some sheep and cattle for meat. Dad says they can swap it for tatties and eggs and diesel at the farm on the way back from town. He says that the animals will die of starvation so it's OK to kill for food.

Mum hears from Granny. Gran says that people are stealing and looting in the cities. Everyone has to walk cause the streets can't take cars or buses now. The Moncreiffs are staying with Granny and Gramps because their house has broken heating. Dad says they can play all the bridge they want! I hope it stops snowing and being cold soon. There's a train stuck in England and the people on it have been stuck for days, and some are dead in the train.

Here is the six o'clock news from the BBC on Wednesday, the fifteenth of January. The Headlines. Britain is still in the grip of cold and snow. Police are struggling to contain the extensive looting taking place in large towns and cities. Many hospitals are relying on generators to supply their electricity but many people are unable to reach the hospitals. The Department of Health estimates that there have been several thousand extra deaths due to the Emergency. The Weather Centre says that there is to be no change until February.

It's Wednesday the fifteenth. Mum had a phone call from Granny. She says the people are catching dogs and cats for food. I think that's horrible, but Dad is doing the same with cattle and sheep. He, Sam, and the keeper have been back to town. They get some food from the shed at Chippies, and tatties and eggs from the farmer. He gets deer and cattle as a swap. He can also give us diesel. Dad says it's a bit like us swapping toys and sweets at the school. Hall school is all right. Some of the people in the Hall sit in on lessons – they talk to the teachers in class and make jokes! At proper school we would be up to see Mrs Winning in a flash if we tried that! The German classes are good! I was frightened of Dieter, but he tells us stories in German and then translates them to English. Some stories are very exciting! Jean Munro does something the same in English. She tells us a very short story and then we have to make it fuller; 'embellish it', is how she puts it. When she gets them in, they get read out then she reads a piece by a famous writer on the same story. Those ones are always better than ours. I asked Mrs Partridge about global warming and why we had got colder. She said that the Gulf Stream has moved to the West and cold air is coming from Russia to meet warm wet air above us. That's what makes all that snow. Dad and Sam are going to try to shift the cars stuck on the hill to be ready for when the thaw comes. Dieter said he would help so the row with Dad must be finished now.

SNOW

Here is the local news for Highland Scotland on Wednesday, the twenty-second of January. Bitter snowy weather continues over all areas. Deer have been driven to lower ground and many are being shot for food. Fruit and vegetables are in short supply but some boats are to bring supplies from Glasgow, as and when they are available. Many ill or injured people are dying because they can't get to hospitals. At Balinrigh, there has been an accident while clearing the road. One person is injured and one has been killed.

Twenty-fifth of January. Was it really three years ago that I last wrote in here? I unearthed this diary while sorting stuff from the old house, ready to move up to Sam's. We're doing a house swap. Sam and Emily had theirs all done up and bought ours (which needs a lot of attention). We have theirs which is smaller but much easier to keep. I'm going to University in Glasgow and Mum is to marry Bill MacKay. I'm really pleased for her cause he's a decent guy and the last while has been horrible for her.

I'm not supposed to know but she had a fling with the keeper about a year after Dad was killed. She was miserable and drinking a lot and would have weeping fits when she came back late. The keeper and his wife moved off further north – I don't know if that was because of the affair or not. Mum got a job with the Mace down the road; that's where she met Bill. He is manager of the wee shop and the bigger one in town. Mum was good in the wee shop and really ran it on her own. Seemingly Bill came to supervise more and more as soon as supervision wasn't needed!

Gran and Gramps helped look after Wee Bobby after school. They're up here now; they moved after that Mrs Moncreiff died. Luckily Dieter and Gert play bridge so they still have their games. Bridge has no language barriers! Dieter was very upset after Dad was killed. He was in hospital with his broken leg for a while. When he came out, he helped Mum lots with insurance and stuff. He knows about these things as he was a lawyer in Germany. Luckily Dad had an insurance policy so we didn't have to move, and Mum says there's enough for me to get to Uni without too many loans.

Farquhar, my boyfriend, is going to Glasgow as well, and we're both in Arts. I'm to do English and he's doing music at Strathclyde. After Dad was killed I wrote about all the difficulty of funerals after the Big Freeze, and how it made grieving harder in many ways yet gave you a lot of business stuff to do which took your mind off misery for a while. Mum and I had to suddenly grow up then.

Farquhar reckons that climate change is still happening; all the storms about the world seem to be stronger and cause more damage and heartache. My essay was printed in the papers when Miss Maclean showed it to them so I'm hoping to get into journalism after Uni. That'll mean staying away from Balinrigh to work where the papers are but I'll always come back to Gran and Gramps, Mum and Wee Bobby.

When we did the house swap, Mum arranged for me to get a plot of ground. It's at the top of the field, about a third of an acre, which was never any use for grazing or growing. If you stand in the middle, you can see for miles, and it's close to Gran and Gramps. Mum says if you've got a wee bit of ground, you need never be stuck. I may be back in Balinrigh! No better place to have a bolt-hole; no better place to remember Dad from time to time.

I'll leave this diary in the new place. Gran has given me a grand new one for when I'm at the University.

HUGHIE'S BAD DAY

Nan Rice

"Are you sure it's not just three, Mr McCurdy?"

"No, Hughie, it's definitely four. I spoke to you last week about it, and it was three then. Three plus one makes four."

"I'm sorry, Mr McCurdy, but I don't have it on me just now."

"Hughie, you never have it on you." Mr McCurdy sighed from the depths of his sixteen stones and five-feet-four height as he looked up at the tall handsome fair-haired youth who was staring at him in horror. "Hughie, I like you son. You're a nice boy, but you've got to pay your dig money."

"I like you too, Mr McCurdy. If I didn't like you I wouldn't stay here. And I know I have to pay for my digs, but I don't have any money and I don't know where to get it."

Mr McCurdy sighed audibly. "Why don't you get a job, Hughie? Then you'll have money. Then you'll be able to pay your digs. Then you won't have any problems, because then you'll have money. Easy. Get a job. Now you've got till Tuesday."

Hughie stood staring at his feet. This turn of events had come as a shock.

As the landlord turned to leave the room he noticed unusual black scuff marks on the linoleum. "Hughie, what's that?"

"Oh, Mr McCurdy, I'm sorry. It's my new shoes. They keep leaving carbon footprints on the linoleum. I'll clean it up."

Shaking his head in exasperation, Mr McCurdy turned and left the room.

Hughie felt like crying. Nineteen-years-old and his life was falling apart. A month ago he had started in a great job as a disc jockey on a new radio station, hoping someone from Radio Tay would be listening in and discover him. He was sure he would be a star. Sadly, the new radio station had gone defunct after that first night and he didn't know why. Now here he was. Broke. And next door to being out in the street.

He would have to phone his Auntie Jessie. She would know what to do. When he dialled her number and found the phone dead, he remembered it had run out of money. He rushed downstairs and got into his car. The petrol gauge told him there was less than a quarter of a tank.

He started the car and drove to his Auntie Jessie's place in a state of agitation. He rang the doorbell, knowing he would have to wait until she managed to prise herself out of her deep comfortable armchair and amble slowly to the door. Suddenly it opened as far as the security chain would allow. Jessie peered through the gap and stared at Hughie.

"Who is it?"

"Auntie Jessie, it's me. You can see it's me."

"Ah just wanted to make sure it wisnae an imposter. Haud on a meenit."

Hughie heard the chain being jiggled, then the door opened and Auntie Jessie welcomed him inside.

"Whit brings you here, son?"

"Aw, it was the factor, Auntie Jessie. He was wanting his rent. Mind you, I don't think it was the money so much as my carbon footprint that bothered him. He thought it was dirt."

"Whit's a carbon footprint?"

"It's awful complicated. One day they say carbon footprints have something to do with aeroplanes. Jeesy peeps, how can aeroplanes leave footprints? The next day they blame it on climate change. Now that doesn't make any sense either, because when it rains, the rain lasts for a while and then it goes off. So that's a change of climate, isn't it? The rain would wash carbon footprints away, not make them. I think politicians just try to bamboozle us to make us think we're not very bright."

"Ye're lucky tae understaun thae things, Hughie."

"You know, Auntie Jessie," Hughie took up position in front of Auntie Jessie when she returned to her chair, "I was watching *Conan the Destroyer* on television last night and then the news came on in the middle of it, so I had to watch that till Conan came back. The news man said that America and China were the worst countries for causing climate change because they wouldn't do anything about their carbon footprints, so I think that means everybody in these countries must leave more carbon footprints than we do in Dundee. But then, these places are warm and sunny and don't have as much rain as Dundee, so their carbon footprints won't be washed away. But I still don't understand how America and China cause climate change when they don't have so much rain. It doesn't make sense."

Auntie Jessie was gazing intently at him.

"It worries me because I'm frightened the Big Bang happens and we'll all be broken up into smithereens and scattered into outer space."

"Ah thoucht a big bang wis jist a smash on the motorway tae Inverness wi' a lot o' cars and some lorries. Ah never kent they went tae outer space efter it. Ah thocht they were jist moved tae garages."

"Oh, no, Auntie Jessie. Big Bang's a lot more serious than that. I think."

"Whit is it then?"

"I don't know, but if we're all in smithereens I don't see how doctors and nurses would be able to put everybody together again. They have problems coping as it is."

"Dae thae Hughie? How's that?"

"Because last week a man went into a hospital somewhere with an awful bad right leg. The doctor examined him and then cut off his left leg. Then they found they had made a mistake so cut off his bad right leg. Then he had no legs."

"My, that's awfy. He widnae' be able tae get aboot because if he had nae legs he widnae even be able tae hop."

"Auntie Jessie, that was only one man and two legs. Imagine everybody in the whole world being blown up into wee bits. It would be like a giant jigsaw trying to fit all the pieces of all the bodies together. The only thing they could go on is the different colours."

"How dae ye mean, Hughie?"

"Well, just think. People are different colours. If a black man got a white leg attached to him, or if a white man saw he had a yellow foot, they would make racist complaints. I mean, these might be the only parts the doctors were able to find that fitted onto these people. You'd think they would be grateful to have a leg or a foot rather than be without one. The colour shouldn't really matter that much."

"Ah don't think a yellow foot wid bother me, Hughie, because naebody would see it inside ma shoe an' ah don't run in races, so ah widnae complain. But ah don't think ah wid like a black leg. People would think ah hid awfy bad varicose veins."

"Never mind that just now, Auntie Jessie, I've enough to worry me. How am I going to get money for Mr McCurdy?" He looked at her hopefully.

There was silence while they both gave some thought to the matter, then Jessie said, "Ah've heard the Soshul gie money tae onybody that asks fur it. Noo, if they say they canny gie ye rent money jist say ye've a bad back and ye'll get it. Why don't ye go the noo?"

It turned out to be not quite as easy as Auntie Jessie had suggested. The Soshul didn't really seem to exist any more and so Hughie had to go straight to the

Jobcentre. As he drove there a few days later Hughie noticed numerous bottle bins sitting outside houses awaiting collection. That created the embryo of an idea but one that was soon driven from his mind by another problem. He had no money for the parking machine, which meant he had to drive around, with a constant eye on the petrol gauge, to find an out of the way spot to leave the car. Eventually, and feeling a bit uptight, he arrived at the door of the Jobcentre.

The doorman showed him into a long room. Four clerks were sitting several feet from each other at a long desk, separated by glass dividers. Opposite, a queue of eight bored looking individuals were seated in a row, waiting their turn. By the time Hughie received the 'next please' call, he had recovered his equilibrium and rehearsed exactly what he would say. As he approached the clerkess, however, his mind went blank because she was the most beautiful girl he had ever seen. Her short smooth haircut framed a pale round face, and she was delightfully plump and cuddlesome.

"Sit down, please." She gestured to the chair he was standing, open-mouthed, alongside.

Hughie quickly sat then gazed at her adoringly. "Hi. How're you?"

"Fine, thank you. Name please?"

"My name's Hughie. What's yours?"

She chose to ignore the question and asked, "Is that Hugh?"

"No. Just call me Hughie. Everybody does."

"Surname please." Hughie told her his name, address and work experience, all the while attempting to establish a friendly relationship, though with little success. So Hughie waited until she had typed everything into the computer, then pulled his chair forward and placed his elbows on the desk. "You haven't told me your name yet."

The clerkess scrutinized him.

"Julia."

"Julia. Oh, that's a beautiful name. It suits you. I think I'm in love with you."

This comment was ignored as the girl, blushing, busied herself with the computer, and while waiting for her reply Hughie suddenly remembered the bright idea he'd had on the way to the Jobcentre.

"Julia, I'm into saving the planet and climate change and carbon footprints and all that, and I wondered… You know how the Council collects bottles from people without paying for them? Well, what if I collected these bottles and brought them to you and you could pay me?"

Julia moved her eyes from the computer and turned to gaze into Hughie's whilst trying to digest his suggestion. "Hughie, you wanting to save the planet and all is really great. Hold on a minute," and she immediately began typing frantically while Hughie waited on tenterhooks. She hadn't yet said he would get any dosh.

Finally she achieved her objective and turned to him, smiling. "Hughie. We have just the position for you. We have a vacancy in the Waste Collection Department for someone with the same aspirations as you. You could be part of a team, collect bottles to your heart's content, take them to the depot, and get a wage at the end of every week. The money's good. It's a case of 'we help you while you help us'."

Hughie gave the suggestion some thought, then asked, "Is that being a scaffy?"

"No, no. You would be a Waste Collection Technician."

Well, he thought, that sounds all right. "Would I have to wear boots and would they have carbon footprints?"

"Take them off before you go into the house."

"I'm not too keen on working with people because I'm a lone achiever but I'll take it until I can get a Disc Jockey job." He leaned closer to the counter. "Would you like a date with me tonight, Julia? I would take you to Broughty Ferry and Monifieth and show you how the beaches are eroding with the weather and climate change. Then I could take you to Visocchi's for an ice-cream. You would have to pay for it because I've no money. It'll be my turn next week. If you play your cards right you could end up as Mrs McWhirter."

EARTH SUMMIT

Ward McGaughrin

Ben Nevis… conquered
Ben Nevis… a second triumph
Ben Nevis… again
Ben Nevis… the return
Ben Macdui!
Hurrah for climb it change.

Authors' Notes

Who Owns This Land? *by Jessma Carter*, **page 3**

Land ownership has been one of the key factors in Zimbabwe's history, along with greed and corruption. Zimbabwe has great stores of mineral wealth, a good water supply both above and below ground and a benign climate for agriculture and horticulture. All these are being lost. The land is contaminated with pesticides. Chemicals from zinc and copper mining are being discharged into the water systems; rubbish is not collected but burned, creating more air pollution. Large mining corporations and construction companies seem able to bypass any environmental regulations. It is the ordinary Zimbabweans who suffer now – as they did during the cholera outbreak in 2008–9. Long term, Africa may lose one of its most fertile regions.

Flow *by Catherine Young,* **page 9**

I took as inspiration for my story the subject of river catchment areas, in particular stream bank buffer strips and natural flood management (yourcatchment.hutton. ac.uk) These can be fairly small, simple measures that work with nature yet can prove to be very effective.

My stories tend to focus on small, personal moments for characters so I felt this smaller scale subject matter fitted with the tone and themes of my writing. I used the above science topics to mirror the coping technique of acknowledging, feeling and then letting go of strong emotions.

Earth Mither *by Elizabeth Taylor,* **page 16**

Poor field management and excessive cultivation can cause depletion of minerals and soil loss. The constituent parts which contribute to the fertility of the soil are removed and not replaced, leading to poor yields.

Crop rotation has been practiced in various forms since Roman times. A crop which uses one kind of nutrient can be followed by a different one which returns that nutrient to the soil. Fields have traditionally been left uncultivated, or fallow, for a period of time in order to restore fertility.

During the 1930s in the USA and Canada, prairie lands were depleted of fertile topsoil, which blew away in clouds. This Dust Bowl effect was the direct result of failure to rotate crops, allow fields to lie fallow or plant 'green manure' cover crops to retain moisture.

Lost Mountain *by Deborah Williams-Kurz,* **page 18**

While researching the topic of mountaintop removal, I became interested in the plight of Marsh Fork Elementary School in West Virginia, United States. Stubbs Elementary is based on Marsh Fork, which sat 400 feet below a removal site. The impoundment above the school still holds 2.8 billion gallons of coal sludge in its earthen dam. After years of protest, Marsh Fork Elementary has recently been relocated.

Tribunal *by Ed Thompson,* **page 21**

A healthy, sustainable environment is probably a public good i.e. one from which no-one can be excluded, and which cannot therefore be rationed or sold. How then do we ensure that all members of society act in such a way as to meet our environmental goals? This is a Free Rider problem. One solution, depicted in my story, is authoritarian.

Ezekiel *by Stuart Wardrop,* **page 26**

I wrote Ezekiel after reading, and hearing at first hand, some stuff on UN sponsored aid to third world countries. There is no 'conventional' science in it but there is a lot of environmental and social science. Essentially it is about well-meaning but sometimes blundering attempts by the international community to deliver aid. I have fictionalised the country and the tribal names but I'm sure that places like Rwanda/Congo will come to mind, particularly as these countries are seldom far from the news – and usually for all the wrong reasons.

In many third world countries life continues to be cheap, short and nasty and in the short term international aid projects are and will remain essential to survival at one end of the spectrum to progress at the other. In the longer term of course Ezekiel is right when he says that his country must learn to stand on its own two feet – but without the pre-conditions he wishes to impose.

Ancients *by Helen Taylor,* **page 32**

I read an article about the possibility of the Mediterranean drying up at some point in the future and becoming similar to the Dead Sea but on a larger scale, and the concomitant desertification of Southern Europe. It made me wonder how human communities would adapt to this new environment: conceivably an ordered life in shelters where every resource was rationed or a return to a simpler almost hunter gatherer economy. In addition I often wonder what future archaeologists will make of our present day society when they come to excavate its remains.

Luing *by Roderick Manson,* **page 38**
Despite the galloping industrialisation of Scotland's wild places, sometimes human resilience is all you need to find that there are values other than the purely economic.

Tay Beavers *by Roderick Manson*, **page 41**
With the Scottish Government unofficially encouraging the culling of a rare and endangered native wild animal, perhaps said animal might be forgiven for developing something of an attitude!

Moving On *by Cathy Whitfield*, **page 42**
This story was inspired by a recent article in *Scientific American*, 'Global warming: faster than expected', which discusses the global feedback mechanisms which may be driving a period of rapid climate change. It's generally agreed that one of the many effects of climate change will be increasingly severe and unseasonal weather events leading, among other things, to the sort of widespread flooding we've seen in the UK in recent years. This is expected to be exacerbated by the melting of the polar ice-sheets which will result in a global rise in sea-level. Low lying areas will be particularly vulnerable and so I've chosen the Fens as the setting for my short story.

The drainage of the Fens began during the Roman period but the major drainage took place in the late 18th and 19th centuries when steam pumps were employed. Due to shrinkage of the peat following drainage, much of the Fens now lies below high tide level and only sizeable embankments and flood defences stop the land being inundated. Now the climate effects of the industrial revolution that enabled the Fens to be drained may well be reversing the process. But I'm sure people will adapt and my story depicts a man coming to terms with and overcoming personal change as a metaphor for the necessity of mankind in general to adapt to a changing environment.

Hot Air *by Ann Prescott*, **page 47**
My challenge was to imagine the most optimistic outcome of current research interests in a future period when our traditional energy supplies had been exhausted. I also wanted to build on the industrial heritage of Dundee and Fife.

Wind of Change *by Joyce McKinney*, **page 53**
Bill Gammage, in his book, *How Aborigines Made Australia. Prevent Bush Fire the Aboriginal Way*, describes how the indigenous people managed the land with fire.

When early settlers first arrived paintings and written records showed that 'they found a land like a gentleman's estate with only a few trees dotted around rolling grassland'. This was not a natural landscape. It had been encouraged by burning forest to maintain and refresh the grassland. Those fires were small and carefully directed. They called them 'cool fires.' The grasslands were habitat for game and became hunting areas. The Aborigines, by reducing the fuel load, also reduced the fire danger and the trees were pushed up into the mountainous areas.

In present day Australia those grasslands are being covered again by forests for people oppose burn-offs, the population continues to increase and drought becomes an ever-present problem. Fires are now huge and can be unstoppable. Big expanses of land are regularly devastated by fierce and fast moving fires which destroy top soil and the nutrients required for regeneration.

Alfred Howitt in 1890 and Rhys Jones in 1960 spoke of the importance of recognising Aboriginal culture and the expertise in land management they had to offer, but no-one listened. Gammage now delivers the same messages but it does appear that he may be making an impression as the problems of increasing fire hazards become more pressing.

It is an interesting observation that although Australia's population has now multiplied many times over there are far fewer people involved in fire management in the present day than there were before 1788.

Major Incident and the Mooshiners *by Roddie McKenzie*, page 61

Two things inspired this tale. The first was my conscious attempt to write my first comedy and the second was a talk that I attended at Dundee University hosted by CHECR. The speaker put forward the argument that one way of controlling greenhouse gas emissions would be to tax products according to their carbon footprints. Ruminants, including cows and their products, would be heavily taxed under this scheme, as flatulent cows produce 28% of the world's methane release. Methane is twenty-three times more potent than CO_2 as a greenhouse gas. That would be the financial incentive for smuggling 'mooshine'. Reading how drug smugglers in the Caribbean have been caught in home-made submarines established the basis of the plot.

Tilting at Windmills *by David Carson*, page 68

Ever since Don Quixote's fanciful forays, windmills have been regarded as malign or benign, depending on one's point of view, and eyesight. And their modern-day equivalents have probably accentuated this duality. For some people, wind turbines are anathema; for others, they represent a valuable response to the need for renewable and green energy.

My feelings about them are ambivalent. Seen up close, I find they have a majestic and hypnotic quality, accentuated by their rhythmic bass like that of a slow-playing record. As part of a view, however, from the top of a mountain, for example, they look like ungainly gigantic dragonflies caught in and dominating a web of beauty spun by their surroundings.

The Scottish government is committed to green energy creation, and a proliferation of turbines is one outcome. But this is not without consequences for those who wish to profit and those who live in their shadow. And so I imagined a family, living in the not-too-distant future, whose lives come to be controlled by these windmills.

The House *by Fiona Duncan*, **page 73**
This piece was inspired by the idea of an unspecified ecological catastrophe. I'm using this scenario to explore how human beings react to such a disaster.

La Vita È Bella *by June Cadden*, **page 76**
I have always been very keen on recycling so I knew that my story would somehow deal with this aspect of sustainability for our planet. However, how my story ended up is somewhat fanciful and exaggerated though this is perhaps what could happen if someone really got the recycling bug.

The River *by Chris Smith*, **page 80**
The genesis of this piece was the thought of how difficult it is to step over the obvious when writing about climate change. Tempting as the anguish of apocalypse is, I wanted to explore my reaction to the here and now. In a planet populated with serious finger waggers, men with large foreheads and strident evangelists on both sides, my phaser is set to 'smile'.

Roots *by Janice Thomson,* **page 85**
I like nothing better than to wander over our wonderful mountains. But these days it can be difficult to avoid walking by yet another wind farm or viewing a mass of turbines marring a beautiful landscape. The idea for the story came from pondering the future outcome for Scotland should the 'wind farm rush' continue unchecked.

Seaweed and Cotton *by Fiona Pretswell*, page 91

The ideas for this story came from various sources. Initially I was struck by the human resilience part of the work carried out by CECHR. This then developed into thinking about what will happen to us as human beings going forward. Then in one episode of the BBC documentary *Prehistoric Autopsy* they touched on the subject of when we started to have 'humanity' as we understand it today. A pre-Homo Sapiens skeleton had been found that indicated that it belonged to an older woman who would have required support to survive. From this scientists have concluded that even before Homo Sapiens existed, the ideas of society and culture were present in early man. From this I started to think about the question: 'What gives us our humanity?' Finally I started to read *The Selfish Gene* by Richard Dawkins and from the discussion about genes and what certain species do to pass on only the strongest genetic traits I came up with the story of Marcus and his decision.

Lovage Soup *by Catherine Maidment,* page 97

I am conscious of the fragility of nature and how the balance of our environment can be upset by the invasion of alien species, even if Alistair in my story is irritated by what he perceives as red tape. I am also convinced that we have a long way to go to explore the potential medical benefits of plants, native or otherwise.

On an optimistic note, Alistair and Jeanette show resilience and adaptability. They feel their chosen careers have become stale and pointless and they have the courage to risk branching out into something they feel is worthwhile.

A Lovely Day for an Airstrike *by C.B. Donald,* page 101

With this piece I wanted to explore what those of us in the developed north might feel as our lands gain refugees from states that may have become less hospitable, just as ours become more fruitful. I thought that a place like Iceland would be ripe for growth if it just got a little warmer. It's currently almost empty up there, but how would the original inhabitants of these newly populated lands feel if it suddenly got swamped with peoples from around the world? Could they hang on to their identities amidst all of this immigration?

The Cat and the Corn *by J. Stirling*, page 105

My story was sparked off by a small rural town I know which has, very laudably, come together to build its own wind turbine and promote small scale local produce. However I was keen to explore the darker side of the tight-knit community and how it might react when outsiders oppose its plans.

Feeding Time *by Ann-Marie Aslen*, **page 112**

Feeding Time started when I watched a programme about climate change and food supplies. I had no real concept of how fragile our food supply really is and how it can be fatally disrupted by wars, pollution, over-farming and drastic changes in climate. This led me to consider how a collapse in food supply could lead to a complete collapse in civilisation and how far countries would go to survive. This led to a second thought regarding what an alien species might do in such circumstances!

Good Neighbours *by Linda Louden*, **page 117**

Already the summers in Southern England are getting longer and hotter and gardens are suffering. Several counties have seasonal hosepipe bans and there is indeed a hotline to report misuse. Looking at probable controls on future emissions, it is also possible that legal restrictions could be put in place on vehicles which run solely on fossil fuels in an effort to further reduce carbon monoxide production, one of the biggest contributors to global warming.

I wanted to set my story a short time in the future, allowing restrictions on driving petrol engines and on watering plants and lawns to be more rigorously enforced and punished than is current. My characters are regular people, whom we could relate to, law-abiding citizens normally, but whose gardens mean so much to them that they are willing to flout the rules. This is not a story set in an unknown future, but a glimpse of what may happen within our own lifetime.

Snow *by Hamish McBride*, **page 121**

I have been convinced about the coming problem of climate change for some time. A visit to Antarctica, and an association with the Scott Polar Research Institute, made the science of change compelling. I'm sure it won't come suddenly, and I find it interesting wondering just how people will try to cope with forces which will ultimately be beyond their ability to manage. I do think that modern urban life is likely to be less able to cope than older fashioned rural life. Perhaps romantically, I think rural communities will be better placed to show some human resilience than city communities.

Hughie's Bad Day *by Nan Rice*, **page 126**

Climate change is such a vast and varied subject. After several false starts I decided to stick to the basic issues of the carbon footprint which we see advertised everywhere, and bottle collection which we have no option but to take part in. These are two aspects of the subject everyone lives with.

Earth Summit *by Ward McGaughrin*, **page 131**

It's my dad's fault. I have always loved puns. I grew up in a family where I took part in competitive punning with my dad and my two brothers. Dad is still the master and skilfully weaves almost any conversation to a snug fit pun. Even now when two or more of us are gathered together there will always be contrived word-play which may be pun-ishment for others. Obviously with *Earth Summit,* the last line came first.

UNIVERSITY OF
DUNDEE

Courses for Adults 2013/2014 include

- Art & Design
- Art History
- Behavioural Studies
- Botanic Garden
- Business Skills
- Child Development
- Computing
- Creative Writing
- Film Studies
- History & Genealogy
- Image & Text
- Literature
- Opera Appreciation
- Personal Development
- Philosophy
- Poetry
- Psychology
- Reiki
- Science & Nature
- Textile Design

For further information and enrolments please contact

Susan Norrie
Continuing Education
2nd Floor
Tower Building
University of Dundee
Nethergate
Dundee DD1 4HN

01382 381125
conted@dundee.ac.uk
www.dundee.ac.uk/conted